A Soldier's Homecoming

A Soldier's Homecoming

A Glacier Creek Romance

Karen Foley

TULE
PUBLISHING

Chapter One

H E'D FOUND HER.

He'd finally located India Gale, the woman presumably responsible for ruining his mother's life. He'd done his homework, but he'd still had a tough time tracking her down. For a woman who lived in the public eye, he'd uncovered very little about her private life.

Lucas Talbot, recently discharged from the Army, had been back in the United States for barely two months, and most of that time had been spent in New York City and Maine, where her trail had gone cold. He'd had a lucky break when he'd learned she had recently left for Montana, presumably to check out the luxury mountain house she'd acquired as part of the accident settlement.

His family's house.

Just the thought of her living in the home where he had spent the happiest summers of his life galled him. True, he hadn't spent much time in Glacier Creek since he'd graduated college twelve years ago, but he made a point of returning whenever he had the chance to catch up with his two best friends, Jamie Colter and Dylan McCafferty, who both lived in the small Montana town.

The expansive, timber-frame house that had been his stepfather's pride and joy, and where Lucas had spent every summer of his childhood, had sat mostly closed for the past ten years. Lucas couldn't remember when he'd last been inside the house, but that was beside the point. He could handle the house reverting to anyone but her.

Now he sat at a booth in Red's Diner, his coffee untouched, and watched through the window as two women stood talking on the sidewalk across the street. He wasn't much interested in the younger woman, who looked to be no older than his college-aged sisters. His attention was solely for her companion. Not that he could see much of the other woman beneath her wide-brimmed sunhat, dark glasses, and baggy shirt. Even her signature mane of long, black curls was noticeably absent. But there was no mistaking the haughty tilt of her chin, and that's what gave her away. Despite all her efforts to avoid detection, Lucas had finally located India Gale.

He looked again at the magazine article he held in his hand, creased and nearly illegible from repeated folding and handling. The photograph, taken a year earlier, had been clipped from the society pages of *The New Yorker*. It showed a distinguished man in his late sixties escorting a striking younger woman with dark eyes and corkscrew curls, who beamed at the camera. Dressed in a neck-plunging cocktail dress that displayed her gorgeous cleavage, she had a killer body and mile-long legs. Unbidden, Lucas had an image of those legs wrapped around his waist, of the lustrous hair fisted in his hand. He frowned at the traitorous thought and shifted uncomfortably in his seat. He studied the clipping. Her smile was wide, her expression guileless, but Lucas knew better.

As the creative director of *Brazen Magazine*, India Gale led a lavish lifestyle. The tabloids and society pages adored her, claiming she was both the beauty and brains behind the popular women's magazine, responsible for pushing the readership into the stratosphere. But Lucas knew the truth behind her success; she exploited her position and her sex to garner favors and take advantage of unsuspecting men with money and influence.

Men like his stepfather, Martin Howden, a philanthropist, financier, and founding executive of a multibillion-dollar media and entertainment conglomerate, headquartered in New York City.

Late stepfather, he reminded himself.

Lucas had been working a special ops assignment in Yemen when the car wreck had happened. He hadn't been able to return for the funeral, but to hear his mother explain it, Martin would still be alive if not for *that woman*. The medical examiner had concluded that Martin, who had suffered from diabetes, had developed hypoglycemia or severe diabetic shock, while driving. He'd likely lost consciousness, which had resulted in the accident.

None of that mattered to Meredith.

A year after the accident, grief and anger still consumed her. She'd become a wrathful, bitter woman who wanted someone to pay for what she had lost, and her sights were set on India Gale, who had been a passenger in Martin's car on the night of the accident.

Now Lucas watched as the two women made their way slowly down the sidewalk, pausing to admire a storefront beneath a bright blue and white striped awning. A breeze rippled the white fabric of India's shirt, briefly molding it against her body, and then pulling it away again, but not before he saw the lush curves hidden beneath.

Frowning, he turned his gaze past them for a moment. Small, quaint art galleries, gift shops, and restaurants lined Main Street. A long, white banner had been strung across the road, with the words *Glacier Creek Harvest Fest* emblazoned across it, and beneath that the dates of the festival. Where he sat, he could even see the old mercantile building where *Adrenaline Adventures* was housed, and where Jamie and Dylan were likely working.

Two blocks further down, the road ended in a small parking area, before it transitioned into a long, wide pier that extended out over the lake. Small groups of unsuspecting tourists ambled along the old wooden platform as gulls wheeled and dipped overhead, hoping for a handout or an opportunity to pilfer a french fry or other bit of food. Further out, the lake rolled in wind-driven swells, capped in ruffles of white beneath a blue, cloudless sky. Majestic mountains ringed the lake, some capped in snow even now, during the first warm days of autumn. It wouldn't be long before the shorter days and cooler nights transformed the green hues of summer to brilliant shades of red, yellow, and gold. He could see the first hint of the spectacular colors to come.

Returning his attention to the women, he saw they still lingered in front of the shop. Lucas stood and pulled his wallet from his back pocket and tossed a few dollars onto the table, before carefully folding the newspaper clipping and tucking it back inside the billfold.

"Leaving so soon? You haven't even touched your coffee."

He glanced up to see a waitress standing by his table with a steaming coffeepot in one hand. Her name tag read *Audrey*. She was young, probably no more than twenty, and now she gave him a wide smile.

"Are you from around here, Audrey?" he asked conversationally. She was young enough that even if she was, she wouldn't remember him.

"I was born and raised right here in Glacier Creek." She indicated the coffeepot. "I'm just back for the summer job. I go to school in Oregon. Are you here on vacation?"

"You could say that," he replied, and put another couple of bills on the table. "Thanks for the coffee."

Outside, the fresh, mountain air was a welcome balm to

the slow churn of emotions he felt when he saw India Gale.

Resentment.

Anger.

He stood for a moment and inhaled deeply. He hadn't been back in Glacier Creek in nearly ten years, and part of him just wanted to kick back with a cold beer and absorb the beauty that surrounded him. But he was here to do a job, however unwillingly.

He just wanted answers.

He'd promised his mother that much, at least, and no matter how reluctant he was to pursue this, he'd see it through to the end. His plan was to observe India and make his own assessment. If he could engage her and obtain the information he needed, even better.

He'd read the police report. He understood the facts of what had happened the night of the accident. What he didn't know was why his stepfather had been in a car with India Gale. His mother believed they had been having an affair, and she blamed the younger woman for the horrific car wreck that had claimed her husband's life, despite the fact India Gale had been a passenger in the car. She hadn't been the one who'd driven the sports car into a utility pole.

Lucas thought his mother might have been able to get past her grief if India's lawyers had only gone after Martin's insurance money. Instead, they had gone after Martin's personal estate, claiming wrongful injury and damages, as well as pain and suffering for their client. Martin's insurance money should have been enough, but the lawyers had gone after his substantial bank accounts. In order to avoid a protracted trial, unwanted media attention, and hundreds of thousands of dollars in legal fees, they had settled out of court. India Gale had walked away with a financial settlement of fifty million dollars, and the deed to the Montana house.

Lucas didn't begrudge India the money for her pain and suffering. His stepfather had been behind the wheel of the sports car that night, and India had remained in the hospital for months following the accident. He didn't know what specific injuries she'd suffered, but acknowledged she was entitled to compensation. But looking at her now, Lucas couldn't see any lingering evidence of injury. She seemed whole and healthy.

His mother, Meredith Howden, believed herself to be the true victim in this entire, sordid affair. Not only had she lost her husband, she'd also lost everything she'd believed him to be—a faithful and loving partner. Then the lawyers had come knocking, and she'd been forced to liquidate assets.

She'd kept the house in the Hamptons and a vacation house in California but had finally offered to turn over the deed to the house in Montana, valued at more than twenty million dollars. His mother had disliked both Montana and the massive timber-frame house and had spent as little time there as possible when Lucas was a kid, so giving up the house probably hadn't been all that difficult for her. But Lucas wasn't about to judge his mother; both her pain and her loss had been real. He just wished she hadn't asked him to act as her private investigator in determining what India Gale's relationship had been with his stepfather.

Lucas loved his mother, but he'd never been blind to her faults. As a parent, she'd been mostly absent, relying on a revolving staff of au pairs to raise both him and his much younger sisters. In retrospect, he hadn't suffered. The nannies he remembered had been young and active, and they had at least made the effort to play with him and teach him the things his mother didn't have the time or inclination for. She'd been more interested in her next spa treatment or social event.

Martin, on the other hand, had taken an active role in his life, from the time he'd married Lucas's mother when Lucas was just five. Suddenly, there were fishing trips and baseball games, even if the fishing was performed from the stern of a private yacht, and the baseball games were luxury box seats at Yankee Stadium, right behind home plate. Martin Howden may have been a billionaire with a corporation to run, but he always made time for his kids.

Lucas still missed the old man.

Now he paused on the sidewalk and pretended to read a tourist brochure of the region, while eyeing the two women. He knew the younger woman was India's sister, Katie O'Hearn. Half-sister, to be precise. As he'd dug into India's past, he'd learned that her mother, Joanna, had been married three times. She'd had India with her first husband, Alejandro Cordoza before the marriage had ended in divorce. Fourteen years later, she'd had Katie with John O'Hearn. Her third marriage, to Ray Sullivan, had lasted only a year before it, too, had ended in divorce. Now he watched as the two women entered a small shop. Even from where he stood, he heard the soft jangle of bells as they opened the door and disappeared inside.

He withdrew a pair of aviator sunglasses from his shirt pocket and slid them on. The polarized lenses sharpened the colors around him, so that the lake seemed impossibly blue and the flowers that spilled over the window boxes exploded with vibrant color. Glacier Creek was just the sort of pretty, mountain resort town that his younger sisters would adore, but they had been little more than toddlers the last time they'd visited Montana. Off the beaten path, with an abundance of charm and picturesque beauty, the little town had a dreamy quality to it, as if the everyday, ugly problems of the world couldn't intrude here.

Lucas had news…they could, and they would.

Crossing the street, he pretended an interest in the shop windows that he passed: an art gallery with enormous paintings of blue and red poppies, a bath and body shop with stacks of handmade soaps and lotions, and a consignment shop jammed full of eclectic vintage finds.

He paused at the door where the two women had entered. A verdigris copper mermaid hung suspended from the ceiling behind the glass, her hands beckoning shoppers to come inside. Beneath the copper mermaid was an artful display of jewelry and trinkets, small handbags and pretty scarves. He pushed open the door, and the bells overhead tinkled.

Inside, the air was fragrant with a light, floral scent and upbeat pop music played overhead. Lucas removed his sunglasses. The shop was long and narrow, with wide pine flooring and exposed brick walls, and so many display racks of feminine accessories and knickknacks that Lucas felt like a bull in a china shop. He was too big, too broad to move easily amongst the fragile items. He heard the murmur of soft voices at the back of the store and made his way carefully in that direction.

India Gale and her younger sister stood with their backs to him, inspecting a glass curio filled with jewelry. India had removed her hat, and Lucas saw with a sense of surprise that she had cut her long hair, and now it sat tightly around her head in short, springy curls. The collar of her cotton shirt had been turned up, covering the back of her neck, and gold earrings swung from her earlobes, catching the light as she bent to peer more closely at something.

"May I help you?"

Lucas turned to see a saleswoman smiling at him from behind a counter. He didn't miss how her eyes lit with interest as her gaze swept over him. She wore a bright summer dress beneath a lightweight sweater, and she preened as she beamed at him.

"Yes," he replied gratefully. "I'm looking for gifts for my sisters."

"I think I can help you," she said, her smile widening as she came around from behind the counter. "How old are they?"

"They'll turn twenty in a few weeks. They're twins."

"How fun, and how nice for them to have such a thoughtful brother," she enthused. "Where are you visiting from?"

"California." That was partly true, if you considered his family had a vacation home in California, but Lucas didn't actually live there. He looked sideways at India and her sister, but aside from a brief glance in his direction, they pretended not to notice him. But as Lucas turned his attention to the saleswoman, he could feel India watching him. Awareness crawled across his skin and made his muscles tighten reflexively.

"I love California." The saleswoman had stopped at a rack of clothing, and now she pulled out a soft cardigan sweater in a shade of deep green, hemmed with tiny copper beads. "This is one of our best sellers. They come in a variety of colors, and they're made locally by a woman who raises her own alpacas."

Lucas raised his eyebrows. "An alpaca sweater?" He infused just a touch of bemusement into his tone. "I don't know…I'm not even sure what size they are. If I get them something too big, they'll accuse me of calling them fat."

He thought he heard a small snort of laughter from the younger woman as she snuck a quick peek at him from over her shoulder. He jumped on it.

"Excuse me," he said, taking a step toward India and her sister. "I'm sorry to intrude, but maybe you can help me." He deliberately didn't look at India, but instead focused his attention on her sister. "I have two sisters just about your age, and I have no idea what to get for them. Is there anything here that you might recommend?"

From the corner of his eye he saw India give the girl a sharp nudge with her foot, and was certain that if he were to look at her, she would be glaring daggers at him. Fortunately, her sister seemed not to care. She turned fully toward him, a smile still curving her lips. Her hair was a pretty shade of strawberry blonde, and up close he could see her eyes were blue. A smattering of freckles across the bridge of her nose made her seem even younger than he'd first thought.

"Well, I think jewelry is always a safe bet." She stepped back and indicated the glass shelf they had been studying. "I really love the silver and turquoise bracelets, and the earrings are super cute, too. Maybe something like that?"

He leaned forward to get a closer look, aware that India edged away from him, but not before he caught her scent. She smelled like light, floral soap and something else; something deeper and more potent. He forced himself to focus on the jewelry, but was acutely aware of her nearness. He hadn't yet looked directly at her.

"Hmm," he mused. "Those are pretty, and I think you're right; my sisters will love them." Straightening, he looked at the saleswoman. "I'll take two of the bracelets. You can choose which ones. Or better yet," he said, turning back to India's sister, "why don't you choose for me?"

At that, India did turn toward him, a frown furrowing her smooth brow. "I don't think—"

"This one," the younger woman said quickly. She selected a bracelet and held it out to him. "And this one. They're similar, but still different enough to tell them apart."

"Like the twins," Lucas said, letting her drop the two bracelets into his open palm. "Thank you. I think my sisters will love them."

He included both women in his smile, but when his eyes met India's, a small shock reverberated through him. He'd been expecting the woman whose photos he'd seen in *The New Yorker*—a woman who exuded self-confidence and strength. A woman who commanded attention simply by walking into a room. A woman whose smile had brought countless men to their knees—including his stepfather. He'd expected her to be beautiful, but he hadn't expected to have an actual physical reaction to her. He felt as if he'd been punched hard in the solar plexus. For a moment, he couldn't breathe.

She was taller than he'd originally realized, with fine

bone structure and flawless skin. Gale wasn't her real sur-
name. She'd been born India Gale Cordoza, but used Gale as
her professional name. Her father was Brazilian, and Lucas
could see her heritage in her wide dark eyes and tawny skin
tone, and the elegant slash of black eyebrows and thick
lashes. Her dark hair in tight, shining curls around her head
emphasized the delicate bone structure of her face and neck.
Her mouth was lush, and for just an instant Lucas imagined
what she could do with those pillowy lips.

In the brief instant when their gazes collided, Lucas saw
something flash in her dark eyes, before she swiftly averted
her gaze to pull her sunglasses from her pocketbook. Disap-
proval?

"Excuse us, please," she said coolly. Taking the younger
woman by the elbow, she steered her toward the door.

"India," her sister complained, "I really wanted to look at
the rest of the jewelry."

"Another time," she replied shortly.

"Thanks again," Lucas called after them.

India paused at the door and cast him one last look before she slid her sunglasses on and stepped outside, closing
the door firmly behind her.

"Here, let me take those for you." The saleswoman retrieved the two bracelets from his hand and moved behind
the counter. "These were also made by a local artisan, and I'll
include a small info card about the artist and the jewelry."

Lucas was still watching the two women as they stood

outside on the sidewalk, exchanging words. They were talking about him, and he could almost guess what they were saying.

"Did I offend her?" he asked, turning back to the saleswoman. "I didn't mean to."

The girl shrugged. "I'm sure you didn't. She just seems really protective of her sister."

"How do you know they're sisters?" Lucas knew they were sisters, but wondered how well known the two women were in town.

"They've been into the shop a couple of times now, once with their mother," the sales clerk said. "I was surprised when I realized they were sisters, because they look nothing alike, but there are so many blended families out there, I'm guessing they have different fathers."

"So, they live here in town." He said it as a statement. He knew where they were staying, but was curious if India had made any impression on the people of Glacier Creek. Did they realize who she was? Did they know she was staying at the Howden property, or the circumstances that had brought her there?

The saleswoman shrugged. "I don't know. I'm guessing they're tourists. Like you." She held out the small bag. "Will there be anything else?"

Lucas paid for his purchase and accepted the bag. "No, thanks."

By the time he stepped outside, India and her sister were

nowhere in sight. Lucas blew out a hard breath and turned in the direction of the mercantile building and *Adrenaline Adventures*. He'd been in town for just two days, but if Jamie or Dylan realized he'd returned and hadn't made the store his first stop, he'd never hear the end of it. Especially since he was part owner of the extreme adventure business.

He still needed to figure out just how much he was willing to share with his friends about his true reason for returning to Glacier Creek. He didn't want to involve them any more than necessary, but neither did he want them advertising his return. He was counting on the fact that most people wouldn't remember him as the rich kid who had spent his summers in Glacier Creek, living in the Howden house. If anyone asked, he was simply Lucas Talbot, former Army Special Ops, here to catch up with his two best friends and finally take some responsibility as the third partner in *Adrenaline Adventures*.

No one needed to know any more than that.

Chapter Two

"I THOUGHT WE were going to have lunch somewhere," Katie complained, as she maneuvered the Land Cruiser they'd rented toward the outskirts of town.

India dragged her gaze away from the passenger window and forced herself to smile at her sister, and said the one thing she knew would make Katie back off. "Maybe another day. I can feel a headache coming on."

Instantly, Katie's expression turned contrite. "I'm sorry. I made you do too much today."

India waved a hand. "Don't be silly. I enjoyed every second of it."

"Even the guy back at that shop?" Katie pulled her attention away from the road just long enough to waggle her eyebrows suggestively at her sister. "He was freaking hot, didn't you think? Did you see his muscles? That square jaw?" She gave a sigh of rapture. "You sure don't see guys like him on the NYU campus."

India smiled at her sister's obvious infatuation. "He's a little old for you, don't you think?"

"I guess." She glanced at India. "He just seemed like the

kind of guy who could handle whatever life might throw his way, you know?"

India closed her eyes. She didn't want to think about the guy from the shop, or how her heart had just about stopped when she'd looked at him. He'd been a delicious, rock-solid slab of a man, with a jaw that looked as if it had been chiseled from granite, and shoulders that rivaled the nearby mountains. He'd literally blocked out all the light in the little shop as he'd stood looking at the jewelry displays.

Katie was right. He'd looked rugged and masculine and thoroughly capable, and when their eyes had met she'd felt a jolt of awareness go through her. His dark eyes had been shrewd and knowing, as if he could see all the secrets she held closely inside her. As if he knew her. That knowing had both attracted and repelled her and had scared her enough that she'd dragged her sister out of the shop.

Had he recognized her? Did he know who she was?

She'd read the gossip in the supermarket tabloids, knew about the rampant speculation surrounding her relationship with Martin Howden. People wanted to know why she had been in the car with him that horrific night a year earlier.

She wished she knew.

If only she could remember, she would come forward and tell her side of the story. But she had no memories of that night, or even of Martin Howden himself. In short, she had no idea why she'd been with a man old enough to be her father, whose net worth could probably settle the national debt. She couldn't recall a single detail about their relationship.

The doctors had assured her the memory loss was normal, considering the severe head injury she had suffered. She had been in a coma for nearly two months following the accident. But there was no guarantee those memories would return, and until they did, India would never know for certain what had happened that awful night, beyond what the police and the medical examiner had pieced together. Martin Howden had gone into diabetic shock and had fainted in the minutes before the sports car slammed into a utility pole.

She had been careful to keep a low profile following her release from the hospital eight months ago. Her childhood town of Stone Haven, Maine, had seemed a likely place to hide out, but the paparazzi had found her there, too. The stress had nearly overwhelmed her, until her mother had finally declared they would fly to Montana and stay at the mountain home India had received as part of the accident settlement.

Her lawyer had arranged everything through a local property manager. He'd assured her that Martin Howden had not stayed at the house in the last ten years but had instead invited colleagues and clients to vacation there in his absence. Since the details of the settlement had not been made public, only the Howden family knew the house no longer belonged to them. The residents of Glacier Creek would not find it unusual to learn three women were staying at the house, and India could finally have the privacy she craved.

"Maybe we can go back into town tomorrow," Katie was saying. "I really did want to look at some of the earrings in that shop, before you pulled me away." She slid a sly glance at India. "Maybe we'll run into your hottie again."

India frowned. "He's not *my* hottie."

But Katie only laughed softly. "Oh, okay. He totally didn't eat you alive with his eyes. I saw the way you two looked at each other. It's a wonder neither of you spontaneously combusted."

India gave a bark of astonished laughter. "*What?* There was no look!"

"Ha. I know what I saw. I didn't see a ring on his hand, so I think it's safe to say he's single. After all, he was buying something for his sisters, not a wife or a girlfriend."

"I fail to see what this has to do with anything," India grumbled.

"Don't you?" Katie asked, her eyes gleaming. "If a guy like him looked at me the way he looked at you, I'd be all over it. I'd hit that so fast—" She thumped her hand on the steering wheel for emphasis.

"Jesus, Katie, I don't want to hear this!" India said, but she couldn't help laughing. "I don't jump into the sack with every hunk who looks twice at me."

"Maybe you should."

This time, India stared at her sister. "Are you kidding me?"

"Not at all." Her hands had tightened on the steering wheel, and a frown puckered her smooth brow. "Why shouldn't you have some pleasure in your life? Nobody would judge you for taking what you want."

While you can.

Katie hadn't said the words aloud, but they hung in the air between them. India dragged in a deep breath. She didn't want to think about her future, or lack thereof.

"Okay," she finally said. "We can head back into town, and if I see Mr. Hottie again—and that's a big if—I'll be friendlier toward him, okay? But he's probably halfway to California by now."

"Perfect," Katie said, and her smile dissipated the gloom that had temporarily threatened to ruin their afternoon. "Did you see the Arts in the Park poster? Every Sunday afternoon there's an instructor who holds art classes in the park. That looked fun—maybe we could join. I know how much you love to paint. Or, at least you used to."

"I don't know," India demurred. "Maybe you should go with Mom. I don't think it's smart for me to be seen too often in town."

Katie made a sound of disbelief. "Okay. Whatever. I get why we couldn't leave the house in Maine; those slimy reporters were everywhere. But they haven't followed us here, India."

India thought again of Mr. Hottie in the gift shop. He had definitely noticed her. "We should still take precautions."

Katie rolled her eyes. "Are you serious? The accident happened a year ago! Your lawyer said the Howden family hasn't been back to Montana in over a decade. Probably nobody here even remembers them. And nobody would ever guess that you'd choose to come here to hide out, right in plain sight in the Howdens' vacation home. That's what makes this so genius!"

"Don't get attached to the house," India cautioned. "I plan to sell it as soon as I can."

Katie gaped at her. "Are you serious? India, why? The house is so beautiful!"

"What do we need with a six-bedroom house? Besides, I'd rather not have anything that belonged to Martin Howden. It just feels wrong."

Katie gave her a sideways glance. "But you're willing to keep his millions?"

India frowned. "I haven't decided what I'm going to do with the money. I mean, who needs fifty million dollars?"

"Trust me," Katie said drily. "That's a drop in the bucket for the Howden family. I doubt they even miss it. And no amount of money could possibly compensate for—"

She broke abruptly off, and India saw how her mouth flattened and her knuckles tightened around the steering wheel.

"Hey," she said softly, and reached over to lay a hand on Katie's arm. "It's going to be okay. The doctors said I might never have any problems."

Katie nodded and dashed away the tears that threatened to spill over. She gave India a tremulous smile. "I know. But it just seems so unfair. I feel like I grew up without you in my life, and now you're back, but—"

She fell silent, but India knew the words she'd left unspoken.

But you have a piece of shrapnel embedded in your brain, and it's inoperable, and if you don't develop a seizure disorder, it could still dislodge and kill you at any time.

The irony of her situation wasn't lost on India. She had millions of dollars at her disposal, and none of it could save her life.

She couldn't blame Katie for feeling bitter. She felt bitter, too. Katie had been born when India was fourteen years old, so they'd always had more of an aunt-niece relationship than a true sister bond. By the time India had left for college, little Katie hadn't even entered kindergarten yet. India barely knew her sister, and now that they were finally spending time together, there was the possibility it could end.

Just like that.

Without warning.

India had seen an endless succession of surgeons, and they had each told her the same thing—because of its location in her brain, the small bit of metal lodged there couldn't be removed. That tiny piece of shrapnel was like a ticking time bomb that could kill her at any moment.

"I don't want you to worry," India said now. "We're together now, and that's what matters."

Following the accident, Katie had dropped out of college to spend time with her sister. India had tried to object, but Katie had been adamant that she could finish school anytime, while her time with India might be finite. She intended to spend whatever time they had left, together.

Time.

India had never thought much about her own mortality, or how much time she might have left on this earth, until the doctors had told her she could die at any time, without warning. Suddenly, each day—each hour—became a gift. Looking back over the thirty-two years of her life, India regretted the time she'd wasted on people and things she didn't really care about. Her former lifestyle now seemed so trivial. The parties, the gala events, the lavish lifestyle she'd once led now appeared so superficial and shallow that she cringed to think of it. In the end, what did any of it matter? And although she'd once been touted as the youngest and most innovative creative director *Brazen Magazine* had ever hired, the board of directors had wasted no time in replacing her following the accident.

She'd left the hospital with one goal in mind: to spend as much time as she had left with the people she loved most in the world. Her mother, who had stayed by her bedside for the entire four months India had been in the hospital, and her sister, whom she barely knew aside from a handful of weekends spent together in New York City. She'd go to her grave weighed down with regrets but spending time with her family wouldn't be one of them.

They'd arrived in the small town of Glacier Creek just two weeks ago, and India immediately knew why Martin Howden had decided to build a vacation home here. The town lay nestled between the sparkling water of Flathead Lake and the thrusting peaks of the Mission Mountains, while its proximity to Glacier National Park and Whitefish Mountain Resort made it a popular tourist destination. The town boasted numerous restaurants and shops, and the lake itself was a huge attraction during the summer months.

Her lawyer, Robert Mullane, had been the one to suggest she leave New York City and spend some time in Glacier Creek. Of course, he'd also wanted to hire a housekeeper, a chef, a personal driver and two security guards to watch over her while she was in Montana, all of which India had adamantly refused. She didn't need anyone to take care of her. She just wanted to live quietly and not draw attention to herself or her family. Robert had told her she was naïve; that she had absolutely no concept of her own wealth, but that wasn't true.

She just didn't care.

She hadn't objected when Robert insisted on hiring a team of lawyers, tax and investment pros to make the best financial decisions for her, but she didn't involve herself in those decisions. She'd make sure her family had enough money to live comfortably after she was gone, but she intended to donate the vast majority of her newly acquired wealth to charity. The first thing to go would be Martin Howden's house in Montana.

As Katie maneuvered the vehicle up the steep, mountain road that led to the Howden house, India looked with interest out the window. There were several other homes on the road, some of them set back behind the trees with long, private driveways. She couldn't help but wonder about these neighbors. Had they known Martin Howden? Were they aware he had died, or that his property had changed hands? If so, she prayed the news was of no interest to them. She didn't think she could endure journalists and reporters swarming her house, the way they had in both New York and Maine.

As Katie pulled into the driveway, India found herself struck again by the grandeur and beauty of the large, timber-frame home. The house sat perched on the edge of the mountainside with unobstructed views of the town, the lake, and the mountains beyond. But despite the luxurious details, including a custom chef's kitchen, an exercise room, and a climate-controlled wine cellar, the house itself felt warm and welcoming. The great room boasted a natural stone fireplace that soared twenty-five feet upward through the vaulted, beamed ceiling. The furnishings were oversized and so comfortable that India had spent many evenings just curled up on the sofa. She thought she could easily spend the rest of her life here, except for the constant, nagging reminder that the house had once belonged to Martin Howden.

Until her memories of the accident—and of Martin—returned, she wouldn't feel right keeping the house. She didn't think she could keep it, regardless of what she learned. The last thing she remembered was attending a board meeting with the other directors at *Brazen Magazine*, and that had been three weeks prior to the accident. Everything between that meeting and the car wreck itself was just a foggy, gray expanse of nothingness. When she tried to remember, panic swamped her, and she would feel as if she'd been cast adrift in a surging sea, with no land in sight. Then the headaches would begin and for several days she'd be forced to lie in a darkened room, feeling nauseous and weak.

She had tried to piece together those missing days. She'd looked through her date calendar, her emails, and had even talked with several former coworkers, but nothing seemed extraordinary about those weeks. She'd come to work each day, stayed late as she always did, had attended several promotional events, had enjoyed dinner with a girlfriend at an upscale restaurant on Madison Avenue, and then had apparently gotten into a car with Martin Howden following the meal.

But why?

She couldn't force the memories; doing so only made her

head pound and her eyeballs ache. Like now.

Walking into the house, the cool, cavernous interior enveloped her in a sense of calm. There was something about the warm, golden timbers overhead, the massive stone fireplace, and the towering windows that soothed her. Maybe it was the dramatic views, or the sense of being surrounded by nature, but India felt at peace within these walls, and knew parting with the house would be difficult.

Her mother, Joanna, came to greet them from where she had been sitting on the deck. She took one look at India's face, and her brow furrowed with concern.

"Are you okay? What happened?"

"Nothing happened," India assured her. "I'm just tired."

"She got freaked out by some guy downtown," Katie said, brushing past her mother. "And when I say he was *some guy*, I'm not kidding!"

India shot a frown at her sister's retreating back. "I was not *freaked out*."

Her mother drew her into the room with an arm around her shoulders. "What happened? Was he a reporter?"

India almost laughed at the concept. No way was that guy part of the paparazzi. He looked as if he'd just come out of general casting to play the part of a badass antihero in some testosterone-fueled blockbuster film. If India had still been the creative director for *Brazen Magazine*, she would have given that guy an obscene amount of money to appear in one of her photo shoots. Maybe she would have featured him on the front cover, bare-chested and staring into the camera with that scary intensity. No doubt that issue would have sold out in a matter of days.

"No," she finally said. "He was in a shop, picking out some trinkets for his sisters." She paused. "At least, that's what he said he was doing."

"But you don't believe it?"

They sat down on the sofa, and India tucked her feet up beneath her. "Honestly, I don't know. There was just something about him." She passed a hand over her eyes. "I think I'm just tired and my mind is playing tricks on me."

Katie came back into the room with two cold bottled waters. She handed one to India, who pressed it gratefully against her throbbing temple. "He was just a really hot guy," she said, and took a long swallow of water. "There was nothing remotely journalistic about him."

"Did he approach you?" Joanna asked.

"He wanted my help in picking out some jewelry for his sisters," Katie said, looking speculatively at her sister. "But he couldn't take his eyes off India."

India frowned at her younger sister, affronted. "Trust me, it was nothing that dramatic."

"Don't believe her." Katie looked at their mother. "I felt like a voyeur."

India recalled the look that had passed between them. Even the recollection of the way those dark eyes had traveled over her caused a shiver of awareness to chase itself across her skin.

"Are you cold?" Joanna asked, and reached for a soft throw. "Maybe I should light a fire in the fireplace. They say the temperatures are really going to drop tonight."

"There's no need to do that on my account," India said, and pulled the throw over her shoulders. "I'll be warm enough here on the couch with just a blanket."

"Did you take your pills?"

India had suffered severe nightmares since the accident. In the dreams, she was once again trapped inside the burning car, with no possibility of escape. The doors refused to open, and she choked on thick fumes as smoke filled the interior of the car. Then flames would begin to lick at her feet. In her dreams, she was always alone in the car, and she always woke up before the flames consumed her completely. The pills kept the nightmares at bay, but they also left her feeling drugged and lethargic.

"I don't need them," she said.

"If you're sure."

"I am." India smiled at her mother, who fussed over her incessantly. "Go back on the deck. I know how much you love sitting out there."

As she plumped one of the pillows beneath her head and pulled the blanket over her shoulders, Joanna and Katie stepped quietly away. India closed her eyes but found she couldn't sleep. Images of the man from the shop played through her mind like a broken film reel. She pictured again the perceptive eyes in the leanly contoured face, the dark hair that brushed his collar and fell across his brow, and the shadow of beard growth on his chiseled jaw. There was absolutely no reason to think he had taken any interest in her, and yet a sixth sense told her he had.

Had her sister been right? Had his interest in her been simple physical attraction? Even if India had found him equally attractive, there was no point in even fantasizing about what could have been.

Because what would be the point?

Chapter Three

"WHY DIDN'T YOU tell us you were coming back to town?"

Lucas heard the underlying bewilderment and accusation in his friend's voice. He and Jamie Colter sat at the long bar inside The Drop Zone pub, enjoying a cold beer and watching a football game on one of the many flat-screen televisions.

"I wasn't sure I'd have time to come out to Montana," Lucas hedged. "Things have been pretty rough on my mother and the girls, so I wanted to be there for them, especially since I couldn't get home for the funeral last year."

"Man, what happened to Martin totally sucks," Jamie sympathized. "I'm sorry for your loss. He was a good guy."

"He was, yeah."

They were quiet for a moment, lost in recollection. Lucas had no memory of his biological father, who had died in a private plane crash when Lucas was just a toddler. Three years later, when Lucas was barely five, his mother had married billionaire Martin Howden. Martin had been the only father he'd ever known, and he'd been good to Lucas.

Even if they hadn't seen eye-to-eye on most topics, Martin had treated him like a true son.

"How is your mom holding up?" Jamie asked.

Lucas lifted his shoulders. "She's having a hard time. She's angry, having trouble accepting what happened."

Jamie nodded sympathetically. "I'm sure it's difficult for all of you. Are you staying at the house?"

Lucas hesitated. His friends didn't know the details of the accident, and the terms of the settlement had been kept private. He didn't know how much to share with Jamie and Dylan, or if he should tell them the house now belonged to the woman his stepfather had allegedly been screwing around with when he'd died.

Thankfully, he was saved from an immediate response when Dylan McCafferty strode through the door of the pub. Lucas stood up to greet his old friend, and they clasped hands before exchanging a brief, one-armed hug.

"Hey, man," Dylan said, settling onto the stool next to Lucas. "It's good to see you. I was sorry as hell to hear about your old man."

Despite the fact Martin Howden had been his stepfather, Lucas had always referred to him as his father.

"Thanks," he said now. "How's business?"

"Doing great, and getting busier every month," Dylan said.

The next hour was spent talking about the newly formed extreme adventure company, *Adrenaline Adventures*, as well as Jamie's new baby daughter, and Dylan's recent involvement with a woman who had nearly been run out of town after people mistakenly believed her responsible for starting a wildfire.

Jamie chuckled. "You missed one hell of an exciting summer," he said. "It's good to have you back."

"Are you staying at the house?" Dylan asked. "I've seen a big, fancy Land Cruiser going back forth on the mountain road. That's not your rig, is it?"

Dylan's house was located just down the road from the Howden vacation house. Lucas, Jamie, and Dylan had spent a lot of time there, as kids. Now Lucas realized he couldn't tell them the real reason he'd returned to Glacier Creek. They wouldn't understand his need to uncover India's relationship with his stepfather. Or maybe they would, in which case they would want to help him. He wasn't even certain how deep he was willing to dig; only knew he had promised his mother he would do this thing for her, even though it didn't sit well with him.

What good could possibly come of it? Martin was gone. Proving that he'd been unfaithful wouldn't bring him back. Proving India Gale had been after Martin's money wouldn't bring him back, either. Besides, it wasn't as if the settlement had adversely impacted his mother's life. She hadn't even liked the house in Montana and had only visited twice, under duress. Martin's estate had left her with enough money to last her for several lifetimes. No, it wasn't about the money. It had everything to do with the fact Martin had been cheating, and she hadn't had a clue. For a woman who prided herself on her looks, her pedigree, and her own allure, finding out that her husband had looked elsewhere for companionship or sex had to hurt.

"No, I'm not staying at the house," he finally said. "It's occupied right now—a group of women from New York City."

That, at least, was the truth. Neither Dylan nor Jamie would find that unusual, since Martin had frequently allowed clients and family friends to stay at the house, especially since none of the Howden family spent any time there. Following Martin's death, a local property manager ensured the house and grounds were maintained and, as far as Lucas was aware, continued to do so even after the property had changed ownership.

"Man, that's a damned shame," Dylan said, with feeling. "Seems like you should at least be able to sleep in your own bed when you're here."

Lucas didn't respond. Dylan's words conjured up images he'd just as soon not dwell on. Which of the six en suite bedrooms had India Gale selected? Was she sleeping in what had once been Lucas's bed? His buddies didn't know the house no longer belonged to his family, and now wasn't the time to tell them, not when it would only raise more questions.

"So where are you staying?" Jamie asked. "You're welcome to crash with me and Rachel, but I should warn you the baby isn't sleeping through the night yet."

"I have two extra bedrooms," Dylan added. "You know you can always stay with me."

"Thanks, I appreciate that," Lucas said. "But I'm actually staying down at the lake, at the Snapdragon Inn. I don't want to inconvenience anyone. Besides which, Mia makes a killer breakfast. I'm not ashamed to admit that after a year in the desert eating nothing but MREs, I'm enjoying the pampered life."

Mia Davies, the owner of the Gilded Age era bed and breakfast, was well known in town for both her culinary skills and for treating her guests to a full complement of luxuries. The Snapdragon Inn wasn't cheap, but money wasn't an issue for Lucas. He'd made smart investments, had saved a substantial portion of his military pay, and taken a portion of his earnings to underwrite *Adrenaline Adventures*. He appreciated that he now had a third ownership of the company, but preferred his role to remain strictly financial. He left the day-to-day operations in his friends' capable hands.

"How long are you in town?" Dylan asked.

Lucas shrugged. "I'm not sure yet. A couple of weeks, probably."

"Do you remember Cole Tanner?"

Lucas considered for a moment. "I think so. His family owned the lumber mill just outside of town, right?"

Dylan nodded, and Lucas thought his expression looked pained. "Yeah. The mill burned down this past summer during a wildfire, but they're rebuilding it. Anyway, Cole is getting married in a couple of weeks, at the Snapdragon Inn. If you're still around, you should come. Half the town will be there. Should be a fun day."

"I'd hate to crash a wedding," Lucas said doubtfully.

"Cole and Joy would want you to come," Jamie said.

"Sure, if I'm still here," Lucas agreed.

They each ordered a burger and another round of beers and sat talking while they waited for their food to arrive.

"C'mon over to the mercantile tomorrow," Jamie said. "Dylan and I can show you what we've done with the place."

Lucas had seen the photos but looked forward to seeing the climbing wall they'd built in the center of the three-story building.

"Yeah, definitely," he agreed. "I'm looking forward to it."

"Why don't both of you come by my place for dinner on Friday night," Dylan suggested. "I'll throw something on the grill; it'll be like old times." He looked at Lucas. "You'll get to meet Hayden."

"Are you guys living together?" Lucas asked.

"Not yet," Dylan said, his expression one of frustration. "She rented an apartment in town and she's working at the elementary school. But I'm hoping she'll move in before Christmas."

"I'll bring Rachel," Jamie said. "She's dying to get out of

the house."

Lucas nodded, feeling a little overwhelmed. So much had happened in the few years since they'd last seen each other. Jamie, a former Marine and the youngest of the trio, had been seriously injured in a mortar attack in Syria two years earlier. Now here he was with a wife and a newborn. Meanwhile, Dylan—the confirmed bachelor—seemed serious about the woman he'd met over the summer. His obvious infatuation each time he talked about Hayden Temple was a little hard to watch.

"Sounds great," Lucas said. "I'll bring the booze and the cigars." When his friends were silent, he looked at each of them in dismay. "Wait. You don't smoke cigars anymore?"

Jamie shrugged. "Not since Rachel got pregnant."

"Hayden's not a big fan of the smell," Dylan muttered, but he at least had the grace to look sheepish.

Lucas gave a snort. "Jesus Christ. I came back just in time. You guys have turned into a couple of pussies."

"Like you're going to act any different when you finally meet the right one," Jamie taunted. "Personally, I can't wait to witness that."

"Yeah, well, you're going to have hold your britches. It was a little difficult finding dates out in the desert," Lucas joked.

"Which reminds me," Dylan said, "when do you return to your unit?"

Against the wishes of both his mother and stepfather,

Lucas had attended the Military Academy at West Point. He'd graduated near the top of his class and had successfully passed the qualifications to become a Green Beret. He'd spent the past eight years as a Special Forces soldier, performing missions in every hot spot and shit hole known to man. As a result, he hadn't returned home very often or for very long.

"I'm not going back," he said now.

He saw the shock on their faces. He didn't really want to talk about it, because he still wasn't sure how he felt about leaving the military.

"You're shitting me," Jamie finally said.

"What prompted this?" Dylan asked. "You've wanted to be Special Forces for as long as I can remember."

Lucas shrugged. "There's a lot of stuff going on with Martin's estate, and my mother isn't in a position to make sound decisions right now."

It was only a partial truth, but neither Jamie nor Dylan would ever hear the details of the shit that had gone down in Yemen. A night raid to capture a senior Al-Qaeda leader had turned into a firefight that killed three Special Forces soldiers.

His friends.

His brothers-in-arms.

Men who had trusted him.

But political games and the need for deniability meant Lucas's repeated requests for assistance that night had gone unanswered, despite the fact a nearby intelligence unit could have rendered aid. He and his remaining men had barely managed to escape with their lives, carrying their fallen brothers on their backs. Lucas could still taste the bitterness of the betrayal. He'd sworn that night he would get out as soon as he could, and he had.

As far as his mother was concerned, she really wasn't thinking straight. In short, Meredith Howden was out for blood, and only Lucas's promise to uncover the truth had kept her from hunting India Gale down herself. He'd never seen his mother so distraught or vengeful. Then there were the twins, Lily and Natalie, who had worshipped their father. His sudden death had come as a devastating blow, just when they were starting their freshman year of college. Natalie had decided to take a gap year and stay at home to support her mother. Only now, when she should have returned to school, she was still living in the Hamptons with Meredith and showing no desire to move on with her life.

Lily, on the other hand, had just finished her freshman year at Sarah Lawrence.

Barely.

Lucas had seen her grades, and they were abysmal. Worse, her Instagram feed showed a girl out of control. If the photos were to be believed, she spent most of her time drunk or hung over. While some people would call her spoiled and entitled, Lucas saw her actions as those of someone in grief. He'd made the right choice in getting out of the military and coming home. Now, more than ever, his family needed him. His mother had asked him to perform one last mission, and he'd see it through.

"Can we do anything to help?" Dylan asked, frowning.

"I don't think so," Lucas said. "I just needed to see you guys and check on the house, and then I'll head back to New York."

"So, what are you going to do now that you're out?" Jamie asked.

Lucas shrugged. "I haven't gotten that far."

Thankfully, neither of his friends stated the obvious. Lucas came from a wealthy family. His biological father had left him with a modest trust fund, but Lucas had never used it to support himself. He'd invested the bulk of it, and tucked the rest away for a rainy day, the way he'd done with his military pay. His mother would be happy to support him, but enjoying a life of idle luxury had never appealed to him. He needed to be challenged, both mentally and physically. More than that, he needed a sense of purpose. The Army had provided all of that, and more, until suddenly it hadn't. Better to find a new path than to continue along one he no longer trusted.

Jamie had been lucky. When his injuries had forced him into a medical discharge from the Marines, he'd thrown himself into the task of getting *Adrenaline Adventures* up and running with Dylan. Now he traveled around the country, scoping out new locations for their adventure packages, and occasionally leading a white-water rafting trip or scuba diving adventure. He certainly showed no signs of missing the military. If anything, he seemed disgustingly satisfied with his new life.

Lucas, on the other hand, had absolutely no clue what he would do once his present mission—India Gale—was finished. He was prevented from having to provide any further details about his future plans by the arrival of their burgers, and another round of beers. After that, the conversation turned to football and the televised game, and if the Seahawks had a chance of going to the playoffs that season.

By the time they finished their meals and Lucas left The Drop Zone, it was nearly nine o'clock and darkness had fallen. He enjoyed the drive along the lake, watching as lights blinked on in the surrounding hills and mountains, until finally the turnoff to the inn came into view. The Snapdragon Inn had been built at the turn of last century on a gentle knoll overlooking a private bay on Flathead Lake. During the day, there were sweeping views down the lake to the distant mountains. The inn itself was a sprawling, turreted house with a shingled and stone exterior, and a wide veranda that wrapped completely around the main structure.

As he pulled into the parking lot and climbed out of the car, he saw several guests gathered around a large fire pit down by the water. The firelight encircled the group in a warm, orange glow of light, and the sound of their laughter carried clearly on the crisp, night air.

Tossing his keys in his hand, Lucas climbed the stairs to the front entrance. Someone had placed a dozen or more lanterns along the length of the wide veranda, and several more guests sat on the porch enjoying cocktails by the soft lighting.

"Hi, Lucas."

Lucas turned to see Mia rise from one of the rockers and walk toward him. A strikingly pretty woman with sleek dark hair and dark eyes, she owned the bed and breakfast and ran it single-handedly with some help from her mother. Lucas knew she had grown up in Glacier Creek, but because she had been a few years older than Lucas, and because he had only spent summers in town, they hadn't known each other. As far as he knew, she had no clue about his background or his identity as Martin Howden's stepson.

"Hey, Mia," he said. "Everything okay?"

"As well as can be expected." She pulled a face and lowered her voice. "We're having a little trouble with the electricity right now. Nothing major, but we have no lights. It's an old house, so these things happen."

For the first time, Lucas noticed the entire house was dark. "Anything I can do?"

"No, but thank you. Sam Moreno is inside working on it. He's a local electrician, and I'm so glad he was able to come out here on such short notice." She indicated several vacant rocking chairs. "You're welcome to join us for a cocktail while we wait for the lights to come back on."

Lucas hesitated.

"Or you can grab one of the flashlights here," Mia said, indicating a small porch table, on which several small flashlights had been neatly arranged. "I put a lantern in your room, so you'll have some light."

Lucas picked up one of the flashlights. "Thanks. I hope I'm not being rude if I ask for a rain check on the cocktail."

Mai laughed. "Absolutely not."

But as Lucas turned to go inside, the door swung open and a man came out onto the porch, appearing disheveled and aggravated. He wore jeans and a heavy shirt, and now he removed his baseball cap and swiped a hand over his receding hairline.

"I'm sorry, Mia, but this is going to take a little longer than I originally thought," he said, before he saw Lucas. "Sorry to interrupt."

"Sam, this is Lucas Talbot, one of our guests," Mia said, quickly making introductions. "What seems to be the problem?"

"Looks like some kind of animal chewed through the wiring in the basement," Sam said. "I have some extra cable in the truck, but it's going to be a while before I have it replaced and working."

Mia cast a wary glance at her guests on the porch, and for a moment Lucas thought she might actually *shush* the other man. Before Sam could reply, his cell phone rang and with a muttered apology, he stepped away to answer it.

"I hope none of my other guests overheard that," Mia said in a whisper. "I'd hate for anyone to think we have a rodent problem. We've never had any issues before."

"It's that time of year," Lucas said, smiling. "The critters want to come inside, where it's warm."

Sam finished his call and came back to Mia's side. "When it rains it pours," he said ruefully. "That was the property manager for the Howden place. Seems like the power in their kitchen just went on the fritz. I told him I'd head up there just as soon as I'm finished here, but he didn't sound too happy. You know how those rich people can be—they want instant gratification."

"Did he say it was the entire kitchen, or just the appliances?" Lucas asked.

Sam sharpened his gaze on Lucas. "Just the fridge and the oven. But how did you know that?"

"I know the house," he admitted. "Listen, if you'd like, I'd be happy to take a drive up there and check it out. I think I know what the problem may be."

"Jeez, I don't know," Sam said, scratching the back of his neck. "I don't want to get in any trouble, especially not with friends of the Howdens."

"I'll tell them I work for you, and you can even submit an invoice and get paid for the job," Lucas said. "But if the problem is what I think it is, it's a simple fix. No tools required. I'll be out of there in about five minutes."

He could see indecision warring on the other man's face,

and finally Sam nodded. "Okay, fine. But if it turns out to be a bigger problem than you originally thought, give me a call and I'll come over." Reaching into a pocket, he withdrew a business card and handed it to Lucas. "Good luck, and thanks."

Lucas tucked the card into his back pocket, and turned away, but Mia forestalled him with a hand on his arm. He looked at her expectantly.

"How is it you're familiar with the Howden house?" she asked.

Lucas saw open curiosity and something that might have been suspicion in her dark eyes. The last thing he wanted was for anyone to realize he was Martin Howden's stepson. Any chance of getting to know India Gale would be gone if she knew who he was. But he also hated lying, especially to Mia.

"I've actually stayed there before, and the same thing happened with the electrical," he finally said, giving her as much of the truth as he could. "Whenever I come to Glacier Creek, that's normally where I stay. But now someone else is there, so here I am at the Snapdragon Inn."

Mia tipped her head to one side as she considered him. "What is it, exactly, that you said you do?"

Lucas grinned. "I didn't. But if it makes you feel better, I know the Howden family very well. I'm not about to run off with their fine silver."

"That never even occurred to me," she said, her eyes

widening in surprise. "Well, hopefully it won't be anything serious. I just feel uncomfortable having you—a paying guest—do something so—"

"Menial?" he supplied helpfully. "I've done worse jobs in my life."

"I was going to say late at night," she replied. "But if you really don't mind, then you're doing me a favor, too. If Sam had to leave in order to take care of the Howden house, I don't know what I'd tell my guests."

"It's no problem," he assured her. "And like I said, it'll probably only take me five minutes."

As he climbed into his rented Jeep and drove the familiar roads that would take him to his family's former vacation house, he couldn't help but wonder what he would find.

Chapter Four

INDIA WAS DOWNSTAIRS, on the lower level of the house, having successfully located the electrical panel in a small anteroom. Everything looked new and each switch was clearly labeled, but no matter how many times she threw the main switch and the one marked *Kitchen*, neither the fridge nor the oven turned back on. If it had been up to her, she would have waited until morning to call an electrician, but both Katie and her mother had been adamant they couldn't let the contents of the fridge and freezer spoil. Thank goodness the property manager had been able to find someone willing to come out at this hour.

"He's here!" Katie shouted from somewhere above her.

India heard muffled voices in the main house, and then the tread of heavy footsteps. She stepped out of the small utility room and into the spacious game room that had been built on the lower level. Even down here, no expense had been spared. A beautifully carved, regulation-sized pool table stood beneath a hanging light fixture, and a fully stocked bar ran the length of one wall, complete with barstools, two flat-screen televisions, and a jukebox in the corner. Comfortable leather seating had been arranged in front of a stone fire-place, and wide glass doors led to another deck with views across the lake. On the far side of the game room, a hallway led to what India knew was the climate-controlled wine cellar, and a sauna.

India listened as the footsteps came down the staircase, and her mouth fell open as the man from the shop—the one she definitely hadn't been thinking about for most of the day—strode into view. As had happened earlier, a small shock went through her. Behind him on the stairs, Katie threw her hands up and silently mouthed the words, *I had no idea.* Then she grinned.

The man stopped when he saw India, and pushed his hands into the front pockets of his jeans. The movement made his broad shoulders bunch, and drew India's attention to the well-defined muscles in his arms. He wore a faded blue T-shirt that hugged the rounded pecs of his chest, and all India could think was that she'd never seen an electrician who looked the way this man did.

Supremely fit.

Capable.

More than a little bit dangerous.

His dark hair looked as if he'd just gotten out of bed, or as if he'd raked his fingers through it. Maybe both.

Never in a million years would she have pegged this guy as an electrician. A builder, maybe. She could picture him on a ladder without a shirt, wearing a tool belt and a fine sheen of sweat. The image caused her inner muscles to clench in a way she hadn't experienced in a long time. Longer than she could remember. She had no business feeling such strong attraction toward this man, and she furiously willed her traitorous body to *calm down*.

"What are you doing here?" she asked now, and her voice came out sharper than she intended.

He didn't look surprised or offended by her less than friendly tone. Instead, a rueful smile tugged at his mouth, and he reached into his back pocket and withdrew a small business card, which he extended toward her.

"Sam Moreno is tied up getting the power back on at the Snapdragon Inn, so he sent me over instead."

He still seemed overly large, even in the enormous game room. Taking a cautious step forward, India retrieved the card from his fingers and glanced at it. "And you are—?"

"Lucas Talbot."

India studied him for a moment. "And you work for Sam?"

"I think I know what the problem is with your electrical panel," he replied. "If I could just take a look?"

His evasive response wasn't lost on India, nor the fact he didn't even carry a toolbox. She opened her mouth to question him further when Katie interrupted.

"Mom said she'll stay upstairs and give a yell if the power comes back on." Behind the man's back, she gave India a fierce look, telling her without words to let the man do his job.

"Okay, fine," she said grudgingly. "The electrical panel is through here, but I've already tried everything."

Lucas Talbot stepped past her into the small anteroom, and India followed him. He was taller and broader than she remembered from their brief encounter downtown, all hard muscles and long legs, neatly packaged in a pair of jeans that hugged his ass and made her unable to stop staring. In the small confines of the utility room, she caught a whiff of something woodsy and clean, and had to resist the urge to step closer and inhale, to see if she could identify the elusive scent.

She watched as he studied the electrical panel and experimentally flipped several of the switches.

"This house was built about twenty-five years ago, on the site of a former hunting lodge," he said conversationally.

"Okay." India failed to see what relevance that had, but decided there was no harm in letting him talk, especially when his voice had such a nice, deep, smoky quality to it.

"Parts of the original structure were incorporated into the current design, but in such a way that you'd never be able to distinguish the old from the new," he continued. Stepping back, he closed the door on the panel, and indicated India should precede him out of the room.

"So that's it?" she asked doubtfully. "You didn't do anything I haven't already tried."

"Follow me."

Without waiting to see if she would obey, he made his way to the wine room. Opening the door, he stepped back to let India and Katie enter, before he reached in and switched on a light, and then closed the door behind him.

India had only been in the wine room once, and although it was a large space, about twenty feet long and nearly as wide, Lucas Talbot made it feel suddenly small. The temperature was markedly cooler in this room, and India felt goose bumps break out along her bare arms. Hundreds of bottles lined the walls, backlit by soft, golden light that provided just enough illumination to move around and read the wine labels. A narrow granite counter ran down the middle of the room, and sported a small sink at one end. Padded stools had been tucked beneath the counter for wine tastings. The room felt almost sacred.

"Why are we in here?" India asked in a whisper.

She watched as Lucas walked to the far end of the room and pressed an unseen lever on the wall. The entire wall swung inward, revealing a dark void on the other side.

"Did you know that was here?" Katie hissed in her ear.

"Of course not," she replied. "But how did *he* know it was here? And what the hell is it?"

Lucas flipped a switch and beckoned India to come forward. When she stepped through the doorway, she realized they were in an old cellar. The floor and walls were constructed of stone, and on one wall she saw an ancient electrical panel with a tangle of wires feeding into round cylinders.

"What is this?" she asked, staring around the small space.

"This is all that remains of the original hunting lodge," Lucas said, peering at the circuit box. "And this ancient fuse box feeds the kitchen appliances, but sometimes it likes to act up."

"Can you fix it?"

He smiled at her, and India felt something catch in her chest. He had a great smile, with even, white teeth and pink gums. But she hadn't expected the dimples. Even beneath the scruff of beard growth they were hard to miss, and those deep indents did something to India's equilibrium. She reached blindly for the doorjamb, missed and stepped back, and likely would have stumbled if Katie wasn't there behind her to lend a supporting hand.

"Hey, Sis, you okay?"

India flushed. "Of course. I just lost my balance."

"Maybe we should go upstairs and let Mr. Talbot finish up down here," Katie suggested, frowning.

India hated the worry she heard in her sister's voice.

"No, I'm fine. Honestly." She turned her attention back to Lucas. He watched her with an intensity that was as unnerving as it was attractive.

"Sure you're okay?" he asked.

The dimples were gone, replaced by a furrowed expression of concern. But at least now she could focus.

"I'm okay. So…what is this, exactly?" she asked, redirecting his attention away from herself and back to the task at hand.

"This is a fifties-era fuse box," he said. "Unlike modern circuit breakers, a fuse can only be used once. When it burns out it needs to be replaced, only it's almost impossible to find replacements these days."

"What can you do?"

With a conspiratorial wink, he reached into the front pocket of his jeans and withdrew a small handful of change. He sorted through it with one finger, finally selecting a penny. He peered closely at it. "Here we go," he said. "A 1981 penny."

"Is that significant?" India asked, bewildered.

"It is, because prior to 1986 pennies were made of 97 percent copper," he said. "That makes them excellent conductors."

India arched an eyebrow. "You're going to use a penny to fix the circuit?"

"Let's hope so." He removed the faulty fuse, and then jammed the penny in where the fuse had just been. "And that should do it."

Even as he said the words, India heard her mother yell from the upper levels of the house that the stove and refrigerator were working again. She stared at Lucas in disbelief, but he just shrugged.

"Like I said, copper is a great conductor." He indicated she should precede him out of the tiny area. "After you."

India made her way back to the main room as Lucas flipped off lights and closed the wine room door. She was acutely aware of him behind her on the stairs. She waited just long enough for Katie to reach the first floor and only when she was sure her sister was out of earshot did she stop on the staircase and turn to face him. Two steps above him, she found herself eye level with him. India realized with a sense of shock that his eyes were green. She'd thought they were brown, but now she could see they were as deep and dark green as the lush pine forests that surrounded Glacier Creek.

"You're not an electrician," she said without preamble. "Who are you, and how did you know about the fuse box behind the wine room?"

To her surprise, he simply tipped his head and considered her for a moment, as if she was a new kind of curious creature that he'd never encountered before.

"I'm sorry," he said smoothly. "You haven't even told me your name."

India flushed. There'd been a reason she hadn't introduced herself. But then, what was the likelihood he knew who she was, or why she was in Glacier Creek?

"I'm India Cordoza," she said simply. "Please answer my questions."

"I've stayed here before," he said quietly. "In fact, I make a point of staying here whenever I visit Montana. Except, apparently, this time."

India continued to stare at him as she processed his

words. Her lawyer had told her that only colleagues or friends of the Howdens stayed at this house. Had this man known Martin Howden, and if so, how well? Did he know about her?

"Did you do business with Martin Howden?"

For just an instant, Lucas Talbot's expression changed. Then he seemed to gather himself, and India wondered if she had imagined the flash of pain in those green eyes.

"No. I'm more of a family friend," he said. "What about you?"

"Did you ask if the house was available?" she pressed, ignoring his question. "What were you told?"

"I don't remember, exactly. Just that the house was already occupied." He shrugged, but she heard the underlying exasperation in his voice. "It was bound to happen, right? Why so many questions?"

"Did you have a problem with the electricity when you were here before?" she asked. "Is that how you knew what to do?"

"Yes, we had the same issue with the fuses, and I remember we used a copper penny to fix it until we could get a new fuse. There used to be a note about it in a guestbook they kept in the kitchen." He gave a careless shrug. "I got lucky. If it had been anything else, I'd have had to ask Sam to come out and take care of it."

"And how do you know Sam?"

"I don't. I'm staying at the Snapdragon Inn, and I was

there when the property manager called, asking if he could come out to get your fridge working. The inn has about twenty guests sitting in the dark. No offense, but their situation seemed a little more urgent, so I offered to come out here and take a look, and Sam agreed."

What he'd said made sense to India, although her heart tripped over itself when he said he was a family friend of the Howdens. How well did he know the family? How well had he known Martin? Could he possibly shed any light on what her own relationship with Martin had been? She ached to ask Lucas all kinds of questions, but the fear of exposing her true identity kept her mouth closed.

"Look, are we done here?" he asked, sounding mildly annoyed. "I agreed to look at your electrical problem, but this is starting to feel like an interrogation."

"Just one more question. Should I get a real electrician out here?" she asked.

"I know enough about electrical wiring to know the copper penny won't burn out, but the wiring might, which could lead to a fire."

"What do you recommend I do?" She chewed her bottom lip in worry. Just the thought of being trapped in a fire caused her insides to clench tightly in fear.

"That's two questions," he drawled, but his eyes held a glint of amusement. "I'd call the property manager and let him know. That's his job, to ensure the house is maintained for safety. He can arrange for someone to come out and update the system."

India nodded. "Okay, thanks. Don't you think it's odd they never updated the system in the first place? I mean, this house is worth millions. Why keep an antiquated fuse box?"

"That's four. Maybe they kept the old system for sentimental reasons." He shrugged. "Hard to say." He indicated the stairs that led up to the first floor. "If you're finished, it's getting late and I should get going."

"Of course." India turned and hurried up the remaining steps, acutely conscious of the big man behind her. Was he looking at her ass? Not much to see beneath the oversized T-shirt and loose pajama bottoms.

Her mother and sister were waiting in the hallway when they came up from the lower level of the house. Now Joanna stepped forward and extended a hand to Lucas.

"Thank you again for coming out at this hour," she said, smiling. "Maybe it seems like a trivial matter, and maybe it could have waited until tomorrow, but I hate to see good food go to waste and that's what would have happened if you hadn't restored the power to the kitchen."

India watched as Lucas shook her hand, and then said his good nights. Although he'd said he could see himself out, she walked with him to the front door and stepped outside onto the front porch, pulling the door partially closed behind her. Lucas paused on the steps, expectant.

"I'm sorry if I was rude to you earlier," she said, crossing her arms against the dropping temperatures. "But seeing you in the shop today, and then having you show up at the house tonight…well, it almost seemed like more than just coincidence."

"It's a small town," he replied, his tone wry. "If you spend any time outside of this house, chances are you're going to run into the same people at least a couple of times."

"Will I run into you again, Mr. Talbot?"

"Call me Lucas. And that depends," he said, "on how long you're planning to be in town, and how often you get out of the house."

"How long are you in town?" she countered.

He hesitated and then took one step back up, toward her. "I'm not sure, yet. If you're interested, I could show you around while I'm here."

"Why would you do that?" She forced herself to stand firm, when every instinct in her body urged her to step back, away from his keen gaze and perfectly honed body.

This time, there was no mistaking the male appreciation in his smile. "You seriously have to ask?"

India felt hot color rush into her face even as an accompanying warmth spread through her center. She only hoped the surrounding darkness concealed her sudden fluster. She might not recall the weeks leading up to the car accident, but she remembered the rest of her life with painful clarity, and her immediate physical reaction to this man was a vivid reminder that it had been a long time since she'd been intimate with anyone—and no matter what the news reports said, India was certain she'd never have slept with Martin Howden.

Lucas Talbot, on the other hand, was blatantly and unapologetically male, comfortable in his own skin and confident of his effect on the opposite sex. She could feel the impact of him all the way to her toes, which were curling inside her slippers.

"That's not necessary," she finally said, her heart rate kicking up at the mere thought of spending any time with this man. "As you said, Glacier Creek is a small town. I think I can say with full confidence that I've seen it all."

"Oh, I doubt that," he murmured, but he didn't press her. He started to turn away, and then seemed to reconsider and turned back to her. "You've asked me a lot of questions tonight, and I've answered them. So here's one for you. What's your relationship with the Howden family?"

It took all of India's control to remain standing on the step and not let her expression reveal her inner panic. After all, it was an innocuous question. Even so, her heart began to pound faster and her palms grew moist. She hated lying, but she would do it in order to protect herself and her mother and sister.

"I'm afraid I'm not at liberty to divulge our relationship," she said carefully.

His eyes narrowed. "Really? That sounds rather mysterious. You're a bit young to be one of Meredith's friends, and a little too old to be hanging out with her daughters."

India drew in a deep breath and smoothed her hands down the front of her T-shirt. "At the risk of sounding rude, Mr. Talbot, my relationship with them is none of your business."

He stilled for just a moment, and India knew an instant of uncertainty. Every muscle in his body seemed to contract and coil in on itself, as if he was a predator preparing to strike. Then he visibly relaxed.

"You're right," he said smoothly. "That did sound rude."

His gaze lingered on her for a long moment before he turned away, lifting a hand in farewell. "Good night, India Cordoza."

She watched him climb into his Jeep, and only when the taillights had vanished into the darkness did she blow out a hard breath, and turn to go into the house, briskly rubbing her bare arms against the chill. She felt as if she'd just faced down a wolf and lived to tell the tale.

Katie waited for her inside the entry.

"Well?" she demanded.

"Well, what?"

"Are you going to go out with him?"

Forcing a brightness to her smile that she was far from feeling, India gave the girl a one-armed hug and pressed a kiss against her soft hair. "Why are you so anxious for me to get involved with a guy I know nothing about?"

Katie shrugged. "Because he's gorgeous? Because...those shoulders? Because he couldn't keep his eyes off you? Because he offered to show you around?"

"Were you eavesdropping?" India asked in mock outrage.

"No," Katie protested, but her eyes sparkled with mischief. "But you were just a little bit rude to him. I think you should call him and make it up to him."

"Yeah, okay," India laughed. "That's not going to happen."

"He obviously wants to get to know you and since he knows the Howden family, he's probably not an ax murderer," Katie pointed out. "Are you going to tell him who you really are?"

India drew back just enough to look at her sister. "Not in a million years."

Chapter Five

"**Y**OU ACTUALLY WENT over there and fixed an electrical problem?" Dylan looked at Lucas, clearly impressed. "How did the current tenants react when you told them the house belongs to your family?"

They were kicking back in Dylan's office on the second floor of *Adrenaline Adventures*, located in the old mercantile building. Two days had passed since Lucas had fixed the fuse issue at the house, and he hadn't seen any sign of India Gale since. He told himself he hadn't spent the better part of those days trolling the downtown streets in the hope of seeing her in one of the many shops or restaurants.

But he had.

He figured someone like India—someone accustomed to the bright lights and excitement of New York City—would soon grow bored cooped up in the mountain home, no matter how luxurious it was. Eventually, she would venture into town. But he'd been wrong.

"I only admitted to staying in the house on previous visits to town, but I didn't tell them who I am," he said now. "In fact, I'd prefer they don't know I'm Martin Howden's stepson."

Dylan sharpened his gaze on Lucas. "Why?"

Lucas shrugged. "People hear the name *Howden*, and you can practically see the dollar signs flashing in their eyes. Or they assume any success I've managed to achieve is only due to my family connections."

Dylan shrugged. "What do you care what they think? If they're staying in that house, it's because they have a shitload of money, too. Right?"

"Probably." Lucas wondered what Dylan would think if he knew the woman staying in the Howden house not only owned the deed to the property, but was also the recipient of a fifty-million-dollar settlement from his late stepfather's estate.

"So what's the problem? You'll likely never see those people again."

"That's just it." Lucas stood up and pushed a hand through his hair. "There's a woman—"

"Ah!" Dylan grinned. "I knew it! Is she staying there, at your house?"

"She is." Lucas only barely managed to keep from grimacing. He couldn't tell Dylan the mountain house no longer belonged to his family without also telling him why. And he sure as hell couldn't tell Dylan how attracted he was to the woman who now owned the house, and may or may not have been sleeping with his stepfather before he died.

"And you didn't know this woman before you met her

two days ago?" Dylan pressed him.

"I knew of her," Lucas hedged, "but we'd never actually met."

"Interesting," Dylan said, trying to suppress his knowing grin.

"What's interesting?" Jamie Colter stood in the doorway of the office, and now he crossed the room to lean one hip on the corner of his desk.

"Lucas met someone," Dylan said, giving the other man a meaningful look.

"Oh yeah? When did this happen?"

"I haven't met someone," Lucas said, frowning. "At least, not in the sense that you're talking about. She's practically a recluse. I'll probably never see her again before I head back to Long Island."

"Oh, man, tell me it isn't Laurel Cavanaugh," Jamie said, his eyes narrowing. "Because she's the only pretty recluse I know of in this town."

"Who?" Lucas asked.

Dylan shrugged. "Laurel is my neighbor. She's not really a recluse, but she hardly ever leaves her house. She writes mystery novels, and she's a bit of a mystery herself. But she's attractive enough, I guess."

"She's more than just attractive," Jamie said. "She's freaking hot. In fact, the only time I've seen Rachel jealous was before we were married, when she thought I was interested in Laurel. Seriously, the chick has a rocking bod, even if she doesn't do anything to show it off."

"It's not Laurel," Dylan said with a smirk. "It's one of the women staying at his house."

"Really! Do you know her through your family?" Jamie asked.

"Something like that," Lucas muttered. "But she has no idea that Martin Howden was my stepfather, and I'd rather keep it that way."

"Oh, definitely," Jamie agreed. "Otherwise, how would you ever know if she likes you for yourself, or for your family connections?"

"Jesus, Jamie," Dylan said in disgust. "He doesn't need to hear that crap."

"No, it's okay," Lucas said. Jamie had provided him with the perfect excuse for why he wanted to keep his identity a secret. Of course, they had no idea that India's net worth guaranteed she'd never need to marry for money. She'd found Martin Howden, instead. "Jamie's right. It's better if she thinks I'm just your average, everyday Joe."

Jamie gave a snort. "Sure. Because who would ever believe a guy with your money would voluntarily join the Special Forces and risk getting his ass blown to kingdom come?"

Dylan cocked an eyebrow and swept Lucas with a critical look. "I don't know…you do have a certain aura of entitlement, and that silver spoon sticking out of your ass is a dead giveaway."

"That's bullshit, and you know it," Lucas said, frowning. "I work for a living, just like everybody else."

"I'm just giving you a hard time." Dylan grinned. "Nobody would ever guess you're stupid rich."

Lucas disliked talking about his family's wealth. He'd inherited a modest amount from his father when he'd died, but he'd never touched it beyond making some smart investments. He felt strongly about making his own way in the world and not living off the hard work of those who had come before him. Had he enjoyed privileges because of his stepfather's wealth and influence? Of course, but he'd never actively sought out those benefits.

Now he looked at his friends, and his tone was serious. "I don't know if this will ever happen, but if the day comes when you do meet India Cordoza, let's just say I'm recently discharged from the Army, and I'm here to work with you at *Adrenaline Adventures*. Agreed?"

Dylan grinned again and reached out to clasp Lucas's hand. "If that's what you want, man. We've got your six."

Jamie pushed himself away from the desk and fist-bumped Lucas. "Agreed. From now on, you're just our down-and-out loser friend."

"Thanks," Lucas said drily. "Are we still on for dinner tonight?"

"We are," Dylan confirmed. "My place, six o'clock. Feel free to bring a friend."

Lucas gave a wry smile. "Thanks, but I'll be flying solo."

He left the mercantile building, glancing at his watch as he stepped outside. It was still early afternoon and the day had turned sunny and clear, but Lucas could feel the cool, crisp hints of autumn in the air.

Glancing down Main Street toward the lake, he could see preparations were already underway for the upcoming harvest festival. Tents and vendor booths had popped up along the center greenway, and a tiered pyramid of scaffolding had been erected near the gazebo to showcase the dozens of jack-o'-lanterns that would soon be on display. Although he knew the festival was an annual highlight for the town, he'd never experienced the event. He'd typically been back in school in New York by the time the festival rolled around.

Thoughts of New York dredged up thoughts of his mother. He would head back to the inn and give her a call. She'd be disappointed with his lack of progress, but he could assure her that he'd at least made contact with India Gale. He wouldn't tell her that the woman was every bit as beautiful as the photos of her suggested. He hadn't been kidding when he'd told India she was too young to be friends with his mother. Both her age and her sultry beauty were enough to ensure Meredith would never have been seen in public with her. He prepared to cross the street to where he'd parked his Jeep, when he heard someone call his name. He paused and saw Katie waving at him further down the sidewalk.

"Hey there!" she called.

Lucas walked toward her, glancing at the sign over the shop window where she stood. *Acker Property Management Specialists.*

"Hey, Katie," he said when he reached her side. "Where's India?"

"She's inside."

"Glad to see she's taking my advice and making sure the electrical service gets upgraded for the kitchen."

Katie looked pretty in a pair of jeans and a loose, flowered top, with her hair pulled back in a ponytail. She swung a shopping bag in one hand and held her phone in the other.

"Yes!" she replied, her eyes widening. "That's totally what she's doing right now! We were out shopping, so decided to stop by and tell the property manager about the electrical problem."

The plate glass window of the office was covered in real estate listings for the local area, making it impossible for Lucas to see through to the interior.

"What are you up to this afternoon?" he asked.

Katie swung her shopping bag. "Not much. Just some shopping."

Lucas gestured toward the office. "Is your sister really making arrangements to have the electrical system fixed?"

Katie looked suddenly uncomfortable. "Yes, of course she is."

Lucas was prevented from asking additional questions when the door to the office opened, and India stepped outside.

"Well, that's taken care of. The house should be listed within the next—" India stopped short when she saw Lucas, and quickly dipped her head to search through the large tote bag she carried over one shoulder. "We meet again, Mr. Talbot," she said, her voice cool. She withdrew a dark pair of sunglasses from the tote and slid them on. "Now I really am beginning to think this is more than coincidence."

"I did warn you that if you venture into town, you're bound to run into people," he said smoothly. "Are you looking for property in Glacier Creek?"

"I beg your pardon?" She gave him a blank look.

Lucas indicated the office behind her, although he already suspected what she had just done. "You mentioned a listing, and this is a property management office, so is it safe to say you're looking for real estate?"

Lucas knew damned well she wasn't interested in buying any property in Glacier Creek. She'd just agreed to list his stepfather's mountain house.

She was selling out.

He shouldn't have been surprised, but the knowledge that she was greedy enough to want even more money both galled and disappointed him.

India looked at him, speechless, and Katie stepped forward.

"Yes, we're looking at a house," she confirmed.

"Which one?" Lucas asked easily.

"There is no particular house," India said quickly. "We're just looking."

Everything in him told Lucas to confront India and call her out on her lies and evasive responses. His stepfather was dead, and she was living a life of luxury in his family vacation house—that she now intended to sell—with fifty million dollars in her bank account. The injustice of it burned him. But he suspected India would vanish again if he challenged her. Wary and aloof, she came across as cold and more than a little unfriendly. But Lucas sensed she was actually afraid. She used a standoffish attitude to keep people at a distance, to prevent them from asking her any personal questions. He needed information, but he also realized he'd need to take a softer approach with her in order not to frighten her away. He'd need to convince her he wasn't a threat.

"You like Glacier Creek that much?" he asked, allowing a hint of skepticism to enter his tone.

"Why not? It's a beautiful town," she replied, tipping her chin up. "But enough about us. What are you doing, besides stalking us?"

Lucas ignored the jab, but didn't miss how Katie gave her sister a sharp nudge. "As it happens," he said, "I was visiting my two friends who own *Adrenaline Adventures*, just down the street. Your sister called out to me as I was leaving, and I came over to say hello."

Katie looked past him to where he indicated. "Really? What sort of adventures do your friends offer?"

"Would you like to see?" He sensed India's hesitation. "If you haven't been inside the old mercantile, it's pretty impressive."

"C'mon, let's go check it out," Katie urged, pulling India forward. "It'll be fun!"

"I guess I don't have a choice," she said, but she smiled as Katie tugged her down the sidewalk.

Lucas knew Katie's sudden interest in seeing the mercantile building was a tactical effort to distract him and prevent any further discussion about their alleged plans to purchase local property. With a small smile, he followed them, admiring the swing of India's shapely hips as she walked. Today she wore a pair of slim-fitting white pants that hugged her hips and showed off her long legs, paired with a denim jacket. She'd turned the collar of the jacket up, and her short curls were mostly hidden beneath a sparkly red cap.

Lucas opened the door for them, and followed them into the cavernous interior of the building. India pulled her sunglasses off and stared, open-mouthed at the climbing wall that dominated the center of the space and rose up three stories to the vaulted glass ceiling above. One side of the climbing wall featured a steep overhang, and they stood for a moment watching a woman work her way to the top, as another climber belayed her ropes.

"That is so cool," Katie breathed. "This whole place is incredible!"

Lucas had to agree. Jamie and Dylan had made the most

of the space, with its brick walls and iron beams, offset by the enormous, industrial windows overlooking Main Street. Kayaks and bicycles hung suspended from the ceiling and walls, and racks of clothing and shelves of equipment filled the first floor.

"There's a travel office upstairs." Lucas indicated the second-story balcony that overlooked the climbing wall and the main floor of the building. "You can look through the brochures, or talk to one of the agents about the kind of adventure you're interested in."

"Hang gliding?" Katie asked hopefully.

"Absolutely."

"What about white-water rafting?" she asked. "Or horseback riding?"

"All of that, and more."

Katie looked at her sister, her eyes bright. "Wouldn't that be fun? I've always wanted to go hang gliding!"

India had removed her sunglasses, and Lucas could see she wasn't enthralled with the idea.

"It's perfectly safe," he assured her. "The guides are all certified and have years of experience in whatever activity you choose."

She glanced again at the people climbing the wall. "I don't know. Life is so short; why take chances?"

Lucas bent his head down and looked directly into her eyes. "You're thinking about this the wrong way. Life is too short *not* to take chances, not to see the wonders of the world, not to live life to the fullest."

She stared at him for a moment, and Lucas saw something in those dark depths that unsettled him. Fear. Indecision. And something that might have been regret.

"You can say that because you've never come close to losing everything," she finally managed, and her voice sounded tight with suppressed emotion. "Taking risks sounds very spontaneous and exciting until you've stood on the edge of the abyss and looked into the darkness, the emptiness. Once you've done that, nothing on earth could induce you to jump."

Momentarily taken aback by the vehemence in her tone, Lucas just stared at her. Katie tried to put an arm around her sister, but India shrugged her off.

"I'm sorry," she said. "It was nice of you to show this to us, but I think it's time for us to head home."

They were interrupted when someone on the balcony called Lucas's name. He looked up to see Dylan standing at the railing. As they watched, he made his way down the staircase until he reached them.

"I thought you left," he said to Lucas, his gaze flicking to India and Katie.

Lucas didn't miss the interest in the younger woman's eyes as she took stock of Dylan. With his impressive physique and long, honey-blond hair, he was a chick magnet.

"I was just on my way out when I ran into these ladies," he said easily. "India and Katie, meet my good friend and part owner of the company, Dylan McCafferty."

Dylan shook each of their hands in turn. "Would you like to give the climbing wall a whirl? Lucas and I can belay for you, it's perfectly safe."

"No!"

The word burst from both women at the same time. Then, aware Lucas and Dylan were staring at them with astonishment, India pulled a face.

"Sorry. That might have been a bit extreme." She turned to her sister. "If you'd like to climb, then go ahead. I'll wait."

Katie shook her head. "Absolutely not. We'll head home, like you said."

"Where are you staying?" Dylan asked.

India hesitated. "We're actually staying at the Howden house, on Mountain View Road."

"No kidding?" Dylan looked deliberately at Lucas, who gave him an imperceptible shake of his head.

"What?" India asked, intercepting the exchange.

"Nothing," Dylan said, smiling at her. "It's just that you and I are neighbors. I literally live in the house next door. You can't see it from the road because the drive is long, but we're the next house as you're heading down the mountain."

"That's, um, very interesting," she said weakly.

"As it happens," Dylan said, "I'm having a friendly, neighborhood barbeque tonight. Why don't you both come over?"

"Oh, no," India protested. "We couldn't intrude."

"You wouldn't be," Dylan said. "In fact, the neighbor on the other side of me, Laurel Cavanaugh, will be there as well. She's our local celebrity, as she writes bestselling mystery novels."

"Oh my God, I've read her books!" Katie exclaimed, and her eyes lit up with excitement. Turning to her sister, she clutched the other woman's arm. "We have to go! Please, India!"

Lucas slid a sideways glance at his friend, who gave him a subtle wink.

"I don't know," India said. "I really don't think—"

"I'm going, as well," Lucas said. "Why don't I pick you both up—and your mother, if she's interested—and we can all go over together?"

Katie still clutched India's arm. "Please? If you don't come with me, then I'll go by myself."

Lucas didn't miss the sharp, warning look India gave her younger sister, just before she relented. "Okay, okay. Fine. We'll go." She turned to Dylan. "Thank you, we would love to join you tonight, as long as we can bring something."

Dylan spread his hands and grinned. "Beverages are always welcome."

"Okay, then." India looked at Lucas. "We'll find our own way there, thanks. C'mon, Katie."

Lucas watched as India took her sister's arm and steered her toward the door. Katie cast them one last, happy look over her shoulder.

"See you tonight!" she called.

"Six o'clock!" Dylan shouted.

And then they were gone.

Dylan crossed his arms over his chest, and arched one eyebrow at Lucas, even as a grin spread across his face.

"That's the woman." His voice was rich with amusement. "Man, you are so screwed."

Chapter Six

D YLAN'S HOUSE WAS also a timber-frame home, and despite the fact it was half the size of the one in which India and Katie were staying, it was equally as charming. Maybe even more so.

India stood on the wide, back deck with her elbows bent on the railing, idly twirling an empty wineglass in her hands as she watched the slow spread of lights winking on in the houses around the lake. She half-listened to the conversation and laughter that surrounded her, but felt little desire to be a part of it. She had only come for Katie's sake, because meeting the renowned mystery author, Laurel Cavanaugh, had been so important to her.

She glanced over her shoulder to where the two women sat together, drinks in hand, deep in conversation. Twinkle lights had been strung over the deck, and under the soft lighting, Katie's face shone with pleasure as she talked to the bestselling writer. India felt a pang of envy.

There had been a time, not so long ago, when India had been the one who others had sought out at parties, the one to cause that look of adoration and wonder on younger women's faces. She had enjoyed going to parties and meeting new people, laughing and flirting and drinking as if she hadn't had a care in the world.

And she hadn't.

She'd had a demanding, stressful, exasperating, thrilling job at *Brazen Magazine*. She'd worked hard, and she'd played even harder. And she'd loved every minute of it. But those days were gone, just like her memories of the accident.

Just like her hopes for the future.

India felt his presence before she saw him. Felt it in the slow spread of awareness across her skin, as surely as if he had stroked a finger along the length of her body. She slid her gaze sideways, to find him standing beside her, watching her with the single intensity she had quickly come to associate with him.

"Are you doing okay?" His voice was low enough that only she could hear him, and she enjoyed the husky rasp of it.

She nodded. "I'm fine. Your friends are nice. Katie's in heaven."

Lucas glanced in the direction of the two women, and smiled. "Yeah, she looks pretty happy." He looked down at the beer he held in his hands for a moment, and then gave her a quizzical look. "But not you."

India pretended to misunderstand. "Not what?"

"You're not happy, and I'm curious why." He studied her face, searching her eyes. "Does it have to do with Martin

Howden?"

India sucked in a breath and stared at him, even as alarm bells rang in her head. "Why would you ask that?"

He shrugged, an insolent lifting of those broad, sculpted shoulders. "Because the few times his name has come up, you've looked ready to burst into tears. You're staying at his family house, which means you either know him or his family, so I thought it safe to surmise that your sadness has to do with his passing." He paused. "Am I right?"

"In a manner of speaking."

"Were you two close?" His voice had gone deeper, had taken on a subtle quality that made India look sharply at him. He couldn't possibly think that she and Martin Howden—

No.

Her mind rebelled against the thought. He'd been married, and she never would have gotten involved with another woman's husband, but until her memories returned, she couldn't say for certain what her relationship had been with the man.

Straightening, she held her empty wineglass up. "I haven't consumed nearly enough alcohol for this conversation."

"Let me take care of that for you," he said. He took her wineglass, holding it in the same hand as his beer bottle, and then indicated she should precede him into the kitchen.

Dylan and his girlfriend, Hayden, were picking at the appetizers laid out on the island while they chatted and laughed with Jamie and his wife, Rachel.

Despite her misgivings, India found she liked both Hayden and Jamie's wife. They were both down-to-earth, friendly women who seemed to accept her on face value. Best of all, they didn't ask a lot of questions.

"Hey, India," Hayden said now with a smile. "Did you bring the shrimp dish? I need the recipe!"

India smiled. "Of course. That's my mom's secret recipe, but I'm sure she won't mind sharing it."

"Why didn't she come with you?" Rachel asked.

"I think she felt this was for young people," India explained.

"That's crazy," Rachel replied. "Please tell her next time she has to come with you!"

"Thank you, I will," India said, but doubted there would be a next time.

She'd already stepped outside her comfort zone by coming over to this party. The more she got to know people, the more they would want to know about her, in turn. She didn't want anyone to know who she was or what had happened to her, at least not until she had figured it out for herself. Then there was the whole financial settlement. How would people react if they knew she was a multimillionaire? Would they treat her differently? And how could she ever be certain they liked her for herself, and not her money? That was just part of the reason why she wanted to donate the bulk of Martin Howden's money to charity. She'd even begun to research centers for head trauma, thinking that might be an appropriate way to divest the funds.

Now Lucas pressed a glass of white sangria into her hand. "Do you know how long you're going to be in town?"

He had asked her the question before, and India had been able to sidestep it. Now, with everyone watching her, she shrugged. "We're not certain. At least through the end of the month."

"Well, that's great!" Rachel exclaimed, looking between India and Hayden. "You'll both be here for the harvest festival."

"I'm actually running a face-painting booth for the kids," Hayden said. She looked at India and shrugged. "I'm the new art teacher at the elementary school, so I thought it would be a good way to get to know people in the community."

"What do you do for work?" Rachel asked, smiling at India.

"I'm, uh, between jobs right now," India said vaguely.

"What did you do at your last job?" she persisted.

India knew she was just being friendly. She didn't want to be rude, but neither did she want to talk about her former job.

"My degree is in graphic design, so I've worked in that field for the last ten years," she finally said.

"Really!" Hayden replied, her eyes lighting up. "My degree is in art and graphic design. What kinds of projects have you worked?"

"Mostly digital media and magazines," she murmured. "If you'll excuse me, I'm feeling tired. I think I'll go tell Katie it's time we were leaving."

Without waiting to see their reactions, she quickly made her way outside, where Katie was still talking to Laurel.

"I'm sorry to interrupt, Katie," she said, leaning over to speak into her sister's ear. "I'm feeling tired and would like to go home."

Katie looked up at her, disappointment on her face. "Really? But we've only been here for an hour. Can't we stay a bit longer?"

"I don't think—"

"Let your sister stay." Lucas had followed her onto the deck, and now he interrupted their discussion. "Dylan and Hayden will be happy to walk her home when she's ready to go."

Katie gave India a pleading smile. "Please? I'm not ready to go, yet. I won't be long, and you don't need to worry about me."

India frowned. "I'm not sure. I hate to impose—"

"You're not," Lucas said.

"But it's getting late..."

"It's barely seven thirty," he replied. "This gang won't break up until at least eleven, maybe later. Katie's more than welcome to stay for as long as she wants."

Even in the indistinct light, India could read the expression in his eyes. He thought she was being unreasonable, treating her sister like a child. He thought she was running away, and he'd be right. She didn't want to talk about herself, or her past. Not with these people, when she didn't know what their connection to Martin Howden was.

"Okay, fine," she finally said. She bent and dropped a kiss on her sister's head. "Don't stay too late."

"I'll walk you home," Lucas said, as they returned to the kitchen.

"You don't need to do that," India protested. "We're literally right next door. I'll be fine."

"I know I don't need to," Lucas said, and a small smile played around his mouth. "But I want to. It's still a good half mile or so. I'd feel better knowing you arrived there safely."

He took her wineglass and set it on the counter, and then waited as India said her good-byes. Outside, the sky was dark, and the air had turned cool. India took a moment to pull her sweater on, startled when Lucas took it from her hands and held it for her, allowing her to push her arms into the sleeves before settling it over her shoulders.

"Thank you," she murmured, acutely aware of how close he stood. "It's getting chilly."

"My car is right here," he said, indicating the black Jeep parked nearby. "I can drive you."

"No, I actually like walking at night," she said, and tipped her head back to look at the sky. "I've never seen stars like this before, so clear and so close."

"They are pretty amazing," he acknowledged. "Where is home for you?"

India hugged her arms around herself as they walked down the long driveway. "Here and there," she said vaguely. "My mother has a house in Maine, and I lived in New York until recently. What about you?"

He slanted her an amused look, and India knew he hadn't missed how she shifted the conversation to himself. "My family has a house in California, but I live in North Carolina. I don't spend much time there. I'm actually thinking about selling and relocating to Glacier Creek and working full-time with Jamie and Dylan."

India couldn't keep the surprise out of her voice. "Really? You like Montana that much?"

"I love Montana."

"What is it that you do?"

"I just got out of the Army. Dylan and Jamie want me to help with their business, so I'm thinking about it."

She looked at him in surprise. She hadn't considered he might have a military background, although it made sense. Now that he'd told her, she could see the soldier in him: the air of command and the self-control. The absolute confidence.

"How long have you been out?" she asked.

"A couple of months."

"Do you miss it?"

He shrugged. "I miss the guys in my unit, but I don't

miss the rest of it—being away from home, getting my ass shot at, and I especially don't miss the political bullshit."

India heard the barely repressed anger in his voice and wondered what had happened to make him so bitter.

"I'm sorry," she said.

They walked in silence for several minutes. When they reached the end of the driveway and turned in the direction of the Howden house, the mountain road grew steep.

"This is a bit of a workout," India said after a moment. She'd spent so much of the past year either in the hospital or recuperating, that she hadn't yet built up any physical endurance. They'd barely begun the incline and already she could feel her calf muscles burning from the exertion.

"You doing okay?" he asked. "Wait here, and I'll go get the Jeep."

"No, I'll be fine." She laughed, albeit a little breathlessly. "I'm just sadly out of shape."

She couldn't help but notice that Lucas seemed not to even notice the steep grade, and his breathing hadn't changed at all. The guy was supremely fit.

"Here, let me help you."

Before India could protest, he took her hand and tucked it firmly into the crook of his arm. Beneath the soft cotton of his shirt, he was layered with muscle and she was close enough that she could feel the heat of his body. She knew she should pull away, but the sensation was so pleasurable that she found herself drawing a little bit closer.

"You said something earlier today that I haven't been able to stop thinking about," he finally said. "Back at *Adrenaline Adventures*."

Inwardly, India groaned. She'd said too much, had revealed too much, and perceptive man that he was, he couldn't let it go.

"I don't remember," she fibbed.

He looked down at her, and the expression in his eyes told her he didn't believe her. "You said taking risks sounds very exciting, until you've stood on the edge of the abyss and looked into the darkness."

India gave a small laugh. "I said that? Well, I was probably just trying to dissuade my sister from doing something too risky. She's young, and she has no sense of self-preservation."

Lucas drew her to a stop, there on the road. Overhead, the stars were brilliant and abundant. The forest on either side of the road was thick and dark, and filled with night sounds. The air was fragrant with pine and damp earth. From where they stood, India couldn't see the lights of any houses, and they might have been a hundred miles from civilization. There was only herself and Lucas.

"What happened to you, India?" His voice was deep, and rasped across her heightened senses. "Why are you so afraid?"

"I'm not afraid." But even her voice, high and breathy, gave her away.

"You are. Not of me, or at least I hope not," he continued. "I'd never hurt you. But I can't help feeling that someone or something has. You're afraid of life. Of living. Why is that?"

India stared at Lucas. He still held her hand tucked against his body, and he was so big and warm and vital, that she suddenly couldn't continue pretending. *She was so tired of pretending.* For just a moment, she wanted to lean against him, to draw on his strength and absorb his energy.

"I almost died in a car accident." She heard the words come out of her mouth before she'd even made a conscious decision to say them.

"Come here," he said roughly.

He pulled her against the solid bulk of his body, and then his arms were around her and her face was pressed against his shoulder. She closed her eyes and breathed in the heady male scent of him and savored the hard strength of his arms around her. Of their own volition, her hands crept to his back and clung to him. They stood like that for endless moments, before Lucas pulled away, putting a small distance between them.

"What happened?"

India shook her head. "Forget it. I shouldn't have said anything; it's in the past."

"You said you almost died, India. How long ago?"

His voice was so low, so compassionate and insistent, that India felt her resolve slip. She'd promised herself she wouldn't tell anyone about the accident, or Martin Howden, or his money, and especially not about her own dim prognosis. But with Lucas, she found herself wanting to tell him everything.

"The accident was just over a year ago," she said quietly, and felt the familiar tightening in her chest whenever she thought about what had happened. "I survived, but the driver...he died at the scene."

Lucas stilled. "I'm sorry."

India nodded. "Thank you."

"Were you and the driver...close?"

India wrapped her arms around her waist. "If you don't mind, I'd rather not talk about it."

She didn't dare reveal any more details about the accident. To do so would risk revealing her own identity, and she didn't know Lucas Talbot enough to know if she could trust him. If he contacted the Howden family and asked about her, he'd soon learn who she was. What if he told someone, or contacted the media? The last thing she wanted was a horde of reporters swarming the house, asking questions she couldn't answer. She knew people assumed she had been having an affair with Martin Howden. Her instincts told her that wasn't true, but until she knew for certain, she'd rather avoid talking about it.

But more than that, she couldn't discuss the accident without becoming emotional. A man had died. Her vivid imagination more than compensated for what she couldn't remember, and she only hoped the coroner had been right when he'd determined the driver hadn't been alive when the car exploded. Any other scenario was just unthinkable.

"But are you okay?" Lucas asked. "How badly were you injured?"

"I'm fine," she assured him. There was no way she would tell him how the sports car had exploded, or about the shrapnel that even now pressed against the base of her brain. She hadn't yet decided what she wanted from Lucas Talbot, but she didn't think she could handle his pity.

But Lucas clearly wasn't done talking about the subject. "Is that why you won't consider hang gliding or rock climbing? Because you want to play it safe?"

India started walking again, grateful when Lucas fell into step beside her, and once more pulled her hand into the curve of his arm. Being physically close to him made it somehow easier to talk to him. But how to explain to him that her reluctance to engage in any risky activities had more to do with the shrapnel, than it did with a fear of heights? The doctors had warned her that a fall or a sudden impact to her head could cause a seizure or worse—the shrapnel to shift or dislodge.

"Let's just say the accident gave me a new appreciation for wanting to do things that won't kill me."

"I get it," Lucas said.

India slanted a sideways glance at him. He'd been in the military, had seen combat. She sensed he understood what she was trying to say. For a moment, he seemed on the verge of saying something, but then thought better of it.

"All I'm saying is that you can't let what happened in your past prevent you from finding joy in your future," he said.

"I'm not averse to experiencing joy," she said cautiously, "as long as it doesn't threaten my life."

In the darkness, Lucas slanted her an inscrutable look. She wished she knew what he was thinking. She had no right to feel this kind of attraction to a guy she'd only just met. She didn't know anything about him except she had an immediate physical reaction to him each time she saw him. He pulled her to a stop on the road but didn't release her hand as he turned to look at her.

"Do you trust me?" he asked now.

The question was so unexpected, that for a moment she couldn't find a response. But her immediate thought was that she did trust him, at least with her physical safety. He radiated confidence, and his entire bearing was one of quiet capability. While she could envision him doing something challenging, he didn't seem the kind of guy who would act recklessly. She sensed he was the kind of man who would put the safety of others before his own. He would assess every situation, determine the risk, and act accordingly. Instinctively, she knew he wouldn't hurt her or put her in harm's way. But she didn't yet trust him enough to share her secrets with him.

"I don't know," she admitted. "I hardly know you. But if

you're asking if I feel safe with you, then the answer is yes. You have nice friends, and I don't think they'd willingly hang out with you if you were an ax murderer."

"Thanks," he said drily. "If you'll let me, I'd like to take you out and show you that you can have some amazing experiences without jeopardizing your safety."

The thought of spending any time with this man was incredibly tempting. He was sexy and smart, and she liked everything she knew about him. But she also didn't know if getting to know him any better was a smart idea. She didn't plan to stay in Glacier Creek and didn't know how fair it was to get involved with someone when she knew they had no chance at any future together. She liked Lucas Talbot. Maybe too much.

"C'mon, India," he said, and reached out to stroke a thumb along her cheek. "What's the worst that could happen? You might actually have some fun and make some good memories."

India looked at him, and knew worse could happen. Much worse.

She could fall head over heels for this guy and his sexy smile.

Chapter Seven

LUCAS THOUGHT INDIA would refuse him, just out of principle. He still couldn't believe she had told him about the car accident, even if she had refused to provide any details. He felt certain that if he could just gain her trust, get closer to her, she would reveal what happened the night his stepfather had died—what her relationship had been with the older man. He owed his mother that much. He'd deliberately opted for a gentler tack with India, and it seemed to be working. He pushed down the guilt he felt at his own deception, reminding himself that he didn't owe her anything.

"Okay," she said now.

"Okay...what?"

India laughed, and her self-consciousness was endearing. Lucas felt like a fraud.

"Okay," she said, peeking shyly at him. "I'll let you take me out and show me some amazing experiences. You've piqued my curiosity."

"You won't regret it."

They reached the end of the Howden driveway, illuminated along the entire length by lampposts, and started making their way toward the house.

"What will we do first?" India asked, as they climbed the steps to the front entrance.

They were standing in front of the closed door, beneath the massive trusses that supported the overhanging roof. A small light hung overhead, and Lucas could see India clearly. He felt a little dazed, as he did every time he looked at her. Her face was a pale oval, framed by her short, dark curls. Her eyes were black pools beneath her winged brows, and her mouth was a temptation he didn't know if he could resist.

She shouldn't trust him.

While he hadn't lied to her outright, he'd lied by omission in not telling her who he was. If she ever found out he was Martin Howden's stepson, she would likely despise him for the deception. But for tonight, with the chilly air turning their breath to misty vapor, and the overhead canopy of the night sky brilliant with a billion stars, all he could think was that he wanted to kiss her.

He needed to kiss her.

If he was honest with himself, he'd thought about her mouth since the first time he saw her in the shop, pursing her lips disapprovingly at him.

"Let's start with this," he rasped softly, and stepped closer.

Her eyes widened, and her lips parted in a soft *oh* of surprise as he slid his hands along the delicate line of her jaw.

Bending his head down, he pressed his mouth against hers. If she gave any indication she was unwilling, he'd back off. She went still for just an instant, and then gave a soft exhalation against his lips, and pressed closer, fusing her mouth to his with an intensity that bordered on desperation. Her lips were soft and hungry, and she tasted like sweet sangria. Her supple body yielded against his. Lucas angled his head for better access and slid one hand to the back of her head, threading his fingers through the silky, springy curls. Immediately, she gave a small sound of distress and broke the kiss.

"I'm sorry," she said, panting, and one hand went to her scalp, where his fingers had just been. "It's just that—" She stared at him, and then stepped back. "I should go in."

Lucas caught her gently by the wrist as she turned toward the door.

"Are you okay?"

"I'm fine."

"Then we're still on for tomorrow?"

She hesitated, and for just an instant Lucas thought she would change her mind.

"Sure," she finally said. "Why not?"

Lucas couldn't deny either the relief or the satisfaction he felt in knowing he would see her again tomorrow.

"Good. I'll pick you up at noon. And don't worry about Katie; Dylan and Hayden will make sure she makes it home safely. Sleep well, India Cordoza."

He walked back to Dylan's house, but he didn't stay

long. Without India, the small gathering seemed less bright, less interesting, and it wasn't long before he said his good-byes, ignoring Dylan's knowing grin.

As he drove back through town, his phone rang. Glancing at the display, he groaned inwardly.

"Hello, Mom," he said, answering.

"Well? What have you learned?" his mother demanded without preamble.

Lucas drew in a calming breath. "Nothing. I've barely met her. If you want me to learn more, you need to be patient."

"Lucas, I've been patient for a year. You've been there for four days. How long is this going to take?"

"As long as necessary," he said. "If I push her for information now, she's going to get suspicious and shut down." He turned onto the lake road that would bring him to the Snapdragon Inn. "I'll be honest—the more I get to know her, the less I like what we're doing. She seems like a genuinely nice person, and she's been through a lot."

Lucas could almost feel the fury that came through the Bluetooth. "*She's* been through a lot? My husband *died* in that accident, Lucas! You weren't here, so you don't know how difficult it was for me. I had to give up the deed to the Montana house to *that woman*! Don't you tell me she's been through a lot! She has fifty million reasons to feel happy. You have no idea what it's been like for me!"

Lucas struggled for patience. His mother liked to remind

him that he hadn't come home when Martin had died, as if he'd had a choice in the matter, which he hadn't. He barely resisted reminding her that she had rarely ever visited the Montana house. "I understand, Mom. I'm sorry. I didn't mean to upset you."

Immediately, Meredith's tone turned contrite and wheedling. "No, I'm the one who's sorry, darling. I hate to sound so bitchy, but you see what this whole sordid affair has done to me. It's *destroyed* me!"

Lucas almost didn't hear her last words because of some background noise that sounded suspiciously like a party. "Where are you, Mom?"

"Oh, I'm at the club. They're having a little get-together, nothing special."

The club, as she so casually referred to it, was the Maidstone Club, an exclusive golf and tennis club perched in the heart of East Hampton, on a secluded stretch of the Atlantic, where wealth, privilege, and pedigree were all prerequisites for membership.

"I'm happy to know you can still enjoy your evening cocktails," he said drily.

"Don't be like that," Meredith said. "The club is one of the few pleasures I have left since Martin died."

Lucas pinched the bridge of his nose. "I have to go, Mom."

"When will you see her again?"

Lucas didn't pretend to misunderstand. "Tomorrow."

"Don't let her hoodwink you, darling," Meredith said. "I know she's young and beautiful, but everything she does is designed to further her own secret, greedy agenda."

Lucas had heard enough. "Okay, I have to go. Have fun at the club."

"But—"

He switched off the phone before Meredith could spill more venom about India. No matter what she said, Lucas couldn't bring himself to believe that India had some hidden motive. If he didn't know about the insurance settlement, he'd have a tough time believing she had any money, never mind millions. She lived frugally, dressed conservatively, and aside from her initial aloofness, didn't really come across as stuck-up or superior. He honestly didn't know what to think about her.

He recalled again how she'd abruptly ended the kiss. He would have sworn she'd enjoyed it, but when he'd slid a hand to the back of her head, she'd pulled swiftly away. Then she'd put her own hand there, almost as if he'd touched a sensitive spot. Had she sustained some kind of head injury in the accident? Is that why her hair had been cut short? Or was he simply creating excuses, where there were none?

He pulled into the gravel parking lot behind the Snap-dragon Inn and killed the engine. The inn looked festively bright, with outdoor lights strung along the length of the wraparound porch, and electric candles glowing in every window. Down by the lake, he could see the glow of the fire pit, and hear the laughter of the guests who congregated there. As he entered the house, Mia materialized from one of the sitting rooms, carrying a tray of glasses. She smiled when she saw him.

"Good evening, Lucas." She indicated the room behind her. "I just set out some snacks and drinks. Tonight is movie night."

Lucas paused. "What's the movie?"

"*Notorious*, with Cary Grant and Ingrid Bergman. Have you seen it?"

He nodded. Lucas had seen the Alfred Hitchcock film several times. "It's a classic."

"So you'll join us?"

Lucas couldn't prevent one, swift glance up the staircase toward his room. "Not tonight. I have some phone calls to make."

"Well, if you change your mind, we're in the library. Feel free to help yourself to some food, or a drink."

"Thank you."

Lucas climbed the stairs to his room, wondering if he should have accepted Mia's offer. He didn't want to come across as antisocial, but neither did he want to spend time in idle conversation with people he didn't know and would likely never see again. If the military had done nothing else, it had given him a limited capacity for useless bullshit. The other guests were nice enough people, but they were also nosy. Just that morning in the dining room, he'd fielded a dozen or so questions from two older couples wanting to know where he was visiting from, what had brought him to Glacier Creek, why he'd come to the inn alone, and on and on. Right now, he was all about India Gale. Everything else was just a distraction.

The lakeside mansion had been lovingly restored, and the woodwork on the staircase and the paneled walls gleamed softly as he made his way to the second floor. His room was one of the larger ones in the inn, with a king bed and a fireplace, and a private balcony that overlooked the lake. He pushed open the doors to the outside, and stood for a moment listening to the voices that drifted toward him from the fire pit, and enjoying the crispness of the autumn air.

He thought again of his conversation with his mother. Initially, he'd been willing to find out what he could about India Gale's personal life because he'd been curious, too, about the woman who somehow managed to get close to his stepfather. He cared less about the money, but understood why the substantial financial settlement bugged the shit out of his mother. On the surface, it made sense that India had been sleeping with his stepfather. Why else would Martin have been alone in his sports car with her? He had a personal driver who typically drove him and his clients around. He rarely took the sports car out, unless it was for his own pleasure. Had India been part of that pleasure?

Uneasiness crawled beneath his skin. He hated thinking

about the possibility of India and his stepfather together; felt a little sick at the images he couldn't keep from streaming through his imagination. She'd kissed him so sweetly earlier. But she'd pulled away before he'd even had a chance to explore her. Had she done it deliberately, to tease him into wanting more?

If so, she'd succeeded.

Chapter Eight

INDIA CAST A cautious, sideways glance at the man behind the steering wheel of the Jeep Wrangler. He'd dressed in a dark blue pullover jersey that hugged the muscular contours of his shoulders and arms and did nothing to disguise his impressive pectorals. He'd pushed the sleeves of the jersey up over his forearms, and she furtively took note of his strong wrists. She couldn't help but stare at his profile, admiring the thrust of cheekbone and chin, the nose that held a hint of arrogance, and his lips... She recalled again the decadence of his mouth, and how his lips had moved over hers, coaxing a response that had surprised even her.

True to his word, he'd picked her up just before noon. She'd all but begged Katie to join them, but her sister had complained she had a headache and might be coming down with something, and had insisted on remaining behind. Not that India believed her. But she couldn't deny she felt both excited and apprehensive at the thought of spending the day alone with Lucas Talbot.

"Is this your Jeep?" she asked now.

"Nah, it's a rental I picked up at the airport. I have an

older Jeep back home that I've been thinking about upgrading, so this is a good chance to see if I like the new model."

The Jeep was big, with four doors and a full-size back seat. Lucas had rolled the canvas top back, to let the wind and sunshine pour over them as they drove.

"Where are we going?" she asked. They'd been driving north, keeping Flathead Lake on their left, until finally they'd put both Glacier Creek and the lake behind them.

Lucas grinned. "We're going to Whitefish Mountain Resort."

"It's a little early in the season for skiing, isn't it?" she asked, even as nervous butterflies took flight in the pit of her stomach.

"Are you afraid of heights?"

"I don't know," she said honestly. "The highest I've ever been is the ninetieth floor of One World Trade Center. I'll be honest; I didn't spend time looking out the windows. I am a little nervous, actually."

"Don't be. You're going to love what I have planned," he said, and shifted his gaze from the road long enough to grin at her.

India stared at him, mesmerized by the deep indents in his lean cheeks. She thought she would likely do anything he wanted, if he would just smile at her the way he was doing now. And that was dangerous, because hadn't she already decided she wouldn't let herself get involved with anyone?

She dragged her gaze away from Lucas and focused instead on the breathtaking scenery that surrounded them. With the open roof, she could appreciate the magnificence of the mountains, and the clearness of the skies overhead. The air was fragrant with pine and moist soil, and India tilted her face toward the sun and closed her eyes for a moment, enjoying the sensation of being outdoors on such a beautiful autumn day. She realized this was the first time she'd really ventured out without her mother or her sister since the accident. She should have felt apprehensive, but realized she felt safe with Lucas.

Soon, they reached the resort town of Whitefish, and India stared, entranced at the sweet downtown. The main street was lined with shops and restaurants, and at the end of the road she could see the majestic rise of the ski resort.

"This reminds me a bit of Glacier Creek," she observed, "only bigger, and with ski slopes."

"Yeah, Whitefish is definitely more of a tourist destination," Lucas agreed. "More hotels and restaurants than Glacier Creek. Which reminds me—are you hungry? I thought we'd have lunch here, first."

"That sounds great," India said, eyeing the many restaurants and pubs they passed.

Lucas drove to a lakeside restaurant with an enormous deck that hung out over the water and afforded stunning views of the mountains that ringed the lake. Despite the popularity of the restaurant and the afternoon lunch crowd, they were seated almost immediately at a small table near the railing, beneath a tiki umbrella. A small reggae band played in one corner of the deck, lending a festive atmosphere to the afternoon.

"This is nice," India commented with appreciation, gazing around. "Have you been here before?"

"No. Dylan recommended it. It's been years since I've been to Whitefish, so I'm not familiar with the restaurants."

He'd removed his sunglasses and now he perused the menu, looking relaxed and so handsome that India wanted to pinch herself. A guy like Lucas Talbot could have any woman he wanted. India hadn't missed the admiring glances he'd drawn from several of the waitresses, and from a group of women having lunch at a nearby table. With his muscular build and chiseled features, he looked masculine and rugged.

"Why are you doing this?" she asked.

He looked up, his green eyes sharpening on her. "What do you mean?"

She shrugged. "Why are you spending the day with me?"

He set his menu aside and leaned back in his chair as he considered her. "You really don't know?"

India's heart had begun a slow step-dance, but under the intensity of his gaze, the tempo increased. "You said that same thing to me the other night, when you offered to show me around town. So the answer is no, I really don't know."

The way he looked at her, so intently, made it hard for India to breathe. He found her attractive, and maybe before the accident she would have understood. But in the past year she had lost weight, lost her long, beautiful hair, and lost the confidence she'd had when she'd worked for *Brazen Magazine*. The days of attending premieres and parties and fashion shows, when she'd drawn nearly as much attention as the main event, were long gone. She no longer recognized that woman. She didn't know if she could go back to being that woman, even if she wanted to.

A slow smile spread across his face, and India felt her insides do a slow somersault. He leaned forward, across the table and his voice dropped low. "Sweetheart, if you can't figure it out, then I must be doing something wrong."

India stared at him for several long seconds, before she dropped her gaze, her insides churning with confused excitement. What she saw in Lucas's eyes made her feel both anxious and thrilled at the same time. For the first time since the accident, she felt beautiful. Desirable. But at the same time, she knew a sense of hopelessness. Getting involved with Lucas Talbot on any level made no sense. Sure, he caused her knees to turn to jelly, and she had an unhealthy fascination with his dimples and his mouth, but even if there was a mutual attraction, it could never develop into anything serious or long-term. Even if she had the courage to tell him about the shrapnel and her own grim prognosis, he'd likely run for the hills. What kind of guy would willingly commit himself to a woman when there was a good chance she would die young?

When the waitress arrived, they each ordered a burger

and a cold drink. Lucas was charming and funny, telling her stories about himself and his friends, Dylan and Jamie, when they were kids, until India's cheeks ached from laughing. The food was delicious, and the tall beer she drank took the edge off both her anxiety and her inhibitions. Afterward, they drove to Whitefish Mountain Resort and parked in the large lot near the base lodge.

"The gondola is operating," she observed, as they made their way toward the lodge. "Is that what we're doing?"

"That's part of it," Lucas confirmed.

India waited while he purchased tickets, and then they stood in line until they were able to climb into a small gondola. India stared out the window of the cable car as it ascended quickly, at a steep incline. As they climbed higher, she could see the entire Flathead valley spread out below them.

"Look," she said, touching Lucas's arm. "There's the lake, and I think I can see the restaurant where we had lunch."

Lucas caught her hand in his and pointed out various landmarks as they rose through the trees, including Glacier National Park to their left. When they reached the summit, Lucas helped her out of the gondola and, still holding her hand firmly in his, led her to a large patio outside the summit lodge, where a beer fest was underway. A country band played lively music beneath a large fest tent. Dozens of beer tables had been set up, along with an outdoor bar, and a dozen or so food vendors sold everything from warm pretzels to burgers and schnitzel.

"Oh, something smells good!" India exclaimed, breathing in the scent of grilled burgers and fried food. "I'm glad we already ate, or I'd be tempted to overindulge here!"

"We'll come back afterward," Lucas promised.

"After what?" She couldn't keep the apprehension out of her voice.

She followed Lucas along a paved trail, and only when she saw the sign, did she pull back.

"An alpine slide?" she squeaked, digging in her heels.

Lucas stopped and pushed his sunglasses to the top of his head. His eyes gleamed. "You're going to love it, I promise."

"Oh, I'm not sure—"

Lucas closed the distance between them and put his hands on her shoulders as he looked into her eyes. "Do you think I would do anything that might put you in danger?"

India chewed her lower lip for a moment, and then shook her head. "No."

"Okay, then. Trust me."

Drawing in a deep breath, she nodded. But when they rounded a curve in the trail and the alpine slide came into view, she balked, pulling on Lucas's hand until he was forced to stop.

"I don't think I can do this," she said, eyeing the slide with uncertainty.

The slide resembled an Olympic luge, and the sleds

themselves were small, barely big enough for one person.

Lucas drew her to one side of the trail and indicated the line of people waiting for their turn. "Look, do you see all those families? There's a mother getting ready to go down with her toddler sitting in front of her."

"They're not even wearing helmets!" India exclaimed in disbelief.

"Because it's perfectly safe," Lucas assured her. "Each sled has a hand-brake, so you can control your speed."

India dragged her gaze from the slide and searched Lucas's eyes, seeing humor and understanding in those green depths. "Will you go behind me?" she begged. "That way, if my sled goes flying off the track, you can at least recover my body."

Lucas laughed out loud, and pulled her into his arms, giving her a swift hug. "That's not going to happen, I promise. You're going to love this so much, I'm willing to bet one ride won't be enough."

India made a grumbling sound of disagreement but couldn't deny his arms around her made her feel infinitely better.

"Why can't they let two adults ride together?" she asked. "I'd feel better if I could ride with you."

"I'm honored by your trust," Lucas said, "but you're going to do just fine."

But when it came time for India to climb onto her sled, she wasn't so sure. From her vantage point, the slide itself seemed impossibly narrow, and descended the mountain at an alarming pitch.

"Place your feet here," the slide instructor told her, "and keep your hands on the brake, here. Have fun."

"Lucas…" she wailed, and then it was too late.

She was flying down the mountain, and the only sound was the soft whoosh of the sled and the wind in her ears. Her heart slammed in her chest, and as the first banked curve came into view, instinct told her to haul back on the brake. She drew in a deep breath and instead modified her speed only slightly, relieved when the sled cruised effortlessly around the bend. After that, she allowed herself to enjoy the ride, taking in the mountain scenery that flew past, and reveling in each dip and curve. All too soon, the end of the slide came into sight, and she drew to a stop. She climbed out of the sled, and then watched as Lucas cruised in behind her.

"So, what did you think?" he asked, as he joined her.

"I think I'd like to go again," she said, laughing. "That was amazing!"

"That's my girl," he said, and before India knew his intent, he bent his head down and pressed a kiss against her mouth.

As kisses went, it was all too brief but it sent bright sparks of happiness shooting through India's body. They rode the alpine slide four more times, until India finally declared she'd had her fill.

"Thank you so much for that experience," she said, as they completed their final ride. "I felt like a kid again!"

"The day's not over yet," he said.

"There's more?"

Lucas laughed. "Oh, India Cordoza, you are so easy."

DARKNESS HAD FALLEN by the time they began the drive back to Glacier Creek. The temperature had begun to drop, and Lucas closed the top of the Jeep. India sat beside him, enjoying the soft country music on the radio, as she replayed the day in her head.

After they'd finished riding the alpine slide, she and Lucas had gone zip-lining, sailing through a canopy of trees while suspended from a cable. The experience had been exhilarating and amazing, as she'd traveled through the trees some two hundred feet above the forest floor. Lucas had been attentive and considerate, allaying her fears and providing words of praise when she completed the course.

Afterward, they'd headed back to the summit lodge where they'd grabbed a glass of cold lemonade, before starting the drive back to Glacier Creek.

"Thank you," she said now, watching Lucas as he drove. "I really enjoyed today. I never would have believed I'd have the courage to do something like zip-lining!"

Lucas pulled his gaze from the road long enough to send

her a swift smile. "I'm glad you had a good time. So, you see? You *can* do adventurous things without risking your life."

India smiled at him, and then quickly looked away. He'd been so kind to her, and it had been so long since she'd done anything resembling normal. In fact, she hadn't even thought about her injury, or what the future might hold, all day. Lucas had no idea about her condition. As a result, he didn't treat her with kid gloves, or hover over her the way her mother and sister did. She hadn't realized how much she missed that until now.

"You've been so generous," she said now, feeling unaccountably emotional. "It's been so long—"

"Whoa, what's going on?" he asked, his expression changing to one of concern. "Are you okay?"

India gave him a trembling smile. "Yes. Better than okay."

He'd given her a perfect day.

The only problem was, now she wanted more.

Chapter Nine

WHATEVER LUCAS HAD expected, it hadn't been the sweet, vulnerable woman he'd discovered on the mountain today. Just thinking about her expression as she'd pushed off the zip-line platform made him smile. Her initial fear had morphed into an exhilarated joy, and her laughter had echoed behind her as she'd zipped away from him. Lucas realized he wanted to hear her laugh like that again, without abandon. He'd started this journey with the single intention of learning more about India. What he'd discovered surprised him. He liked her, and he hadn't expected that.

He thought there was something infinitely sad about India Gale, although she tried to hide it. He could see it in the dark depths of her eyes when she thought no one was watching, and the way her gaze would become faraway, as if her thoughts were somewhere equally distant. Was she thinking about Martin during those moments? Had they been lovers? The thought of her with his stepfather made his gut clench, and he forced the unpleasant images away. The more he got to know India, the more instinct told him she hadn't been romantically involved with Martin. Moreover, his stepfather hadn't been the kind of man who would have looked at a woman outside of his marriage. His vows had meant something to him, even if Meredith had convinced herself they hadn't.

He watched India now as she gazed out the window at the passing landscape. The mountains were dark shadows on the horizon, and the moon cast silvery light on the surface of Whitefish Lake as they drove south. She sighed softly.

"What is it?" he asked. Reaching over, he covered her hand with his. Her skin was soft and warm.

She started and jerked her gaze to him but didn't pull her hand away. "I was just thinking how unexpected this day turned out."

She'd voiced his own thoughts, exactly. He never would have guessed that he would give a shit about this woman. But he did. "In what way?"

She slid him a quick, self-conscious glance. "I didn't expect to like you."

Ah.

He gave her fingers a brief squeeze, before releasing her hand. "I like you, too, India Cordoza."

He liked her too much. Not for the first time, he wished he hadn't agreed to snoop into her life. He wished his mother could move on with her own life, and let the past go. He didn't care about the money that had been settled on India, and he knew for sure his mother and sisters didn't miss it and weren't suffering as a result.

Part of him just wanted to tell India the truth about who he was and see where it went. Maybe she would tell him she and Martin had only been friends, or business associates. Or maybe she would be furious at his deception and shut him out of her life completely. He only knew he liked this woman, and wanted to know her better.

"So, have you decided if you're going to stay in Glacier Creek?"

The question pulled Lucas out of his thoughts.

"I have some things to wrap up in North Carolina first," he offered. "So, I'll head there in a couple of weeks, but hope to be in Glacier Creek full-time by Christmas." He paused. "What about you?"

India gave a noncommittal shrug. "I don't know. Sometimes I feel so confused."

"About what?" He spared her a swift, questioning glance. "India, the world is your proverbial oyster. You're still young, you're smart, and you don't seem to lack resources or family support. So, what's the problem?"

She gave a huff of laughter and passed one hand over her eyes. "You wouldn't believe me even if I told you. Sometimes, I can hardly believe it myself."

Here it was.

She was going to tell him.

Suddenly, he didn't want to know. He wanted to believe that India had simply been in the wrong place at the wrong time. He didn't want to know why she'd been in the sports car that night. He wanted to believe that it had been some-thing as innocent as her accepting a ride home from a friend.

"Hey, it's okay," he assured her quickly. "I'm sure what-ever it is, you'll work it out. You don't need to make any decisions today, right? Today is about having fun, and this conversation just got way too serious."

India nodded and gave him a swift smile, but Lucas thought she seemed relieved.

"Yes," she said gratefully. "Today is about having fun, and today isn't over yet."

Lucas glanced at the digital display on his dash. It was barely seven o'clock, and still early by his standards. "What did you have in mind?"

"I don't know," she said, and gave a surprised laugh. "But I'm not ready to go home yet."

Lucas grinned. "Well, okay then. Still trust me?"

She gave him a tolerant look. "After today, you have to ask?"

Her words should have made him feel satisfied, but in-stead a tight knot of guilt settled into his chest. Reaching out, he found a lively country station and turned the volume up.

"Just to get you in the mood," he said, and gave her a swift smile.

"Hmm, country music? What is it you have in mind, Lucas Talbot?"

"Wait and see, Ms. Cordoza. You're in for a treat."

An hour later, they pulled up in front of The Drop Zone. The local pub was a favorite hangout of the Glacier Creek wildland firefighters and smoke jumpers. The parking lot was nearly full, and Lucas hoped they'd find a vacant spot at the bar, or an empty high-top table.

"Am I dressed for this?" India asked anxiously, as he opened her door and gave her a hand.

"You're perfect," he said truthfully.

Clad in a pair of snug jeans that hugged her hips and emphasized the slender length of her legs, she managed to look both elegant and casual at the same time. She'd paired the jeans with a simple, white, button-down blouse with bright embroidery on the collar and cuffs, lending the outfit a stylish, country look.

Inside the pub, the atmosphere was noisy and cheerful. Lucas saw at a glance that the fifty-foot, carved oak bar was completely full, without so much as one empty stool. Two pool tables occupied the back of the bar, where a vintage jukebox wailed next to a small dance floor. He scanned the twenty or so high-top dinner tables hopefully, and was about to concede defeat, when he heard his name called. Searching the crowd, he saw Dylan stand up and wave a hand.

"This way," he said, and slid a hand beneath India's elbow, steering her through the pub toward a table near the dance floor.

"Hey," Dylan said, clasping his hand. "I thought that was you." Leaning forward, he gave India a swift embrace.

"Nice to see you again, India. You remember my girlfriend, Hayden?"

"Of course."

"Come join us," Dylan said, indicating the two empty chairs at their table.

"Oh, I'm not sure—we'd hate to intrude," India protested.

"Don't be ridiculous," Dylan said, and pulled out an empty stool for her. "We're glad you came in."

India slid into the chair next to Hayden while Lucas summoned a waitress.

"What have you two been up to?" Dylan asked with a grin.

"We went up to Whitefish Mountain Resort and rode the alpine slide, and then did the zip line," India said.

"Did you love it?" Hayden asked.

"I did, actually! I wasn't sure I could go through with it, but it was exhilarating."

Lucas put an arm around India's shoulders and gave her a brief hug. "She had no idea what I had planned until we were there, so I give her a lot of credit for going through with it."

"As if I could have refused," India teased him. "You all but dragged me to the slide."

"Hey—" he laughed "—I wasn't the one who wanted to ride the slide four times!"

"I did love it," India admitted, sheepish, but unable to

prevent the smile that spread across her face.

Lucas stared at her, mesmerized. Thankfully, the waitress arrived, and he ordered a beer for himself while India opted for an iced tea.

"This place has a lot of atmosphere," India observed, looking around her with interest. "I love the tin ceiling tiles!"

"Yeah, those were rescued from a brothel in Taft, which was a former mining town," Dylan offered. "They're embossed with scenes of the gold rush."

"I just love the authenticity of everything," India said. "This place has a really great vibe."

Their drinks arrived, and after a quick consultation, they ordered several appetizers. The jukebox belted out country music, and Lucas saw India tapping the floor in beat to the music.

"Do you want to take a turn around the dance floor?" he asked.

She started, and then blushed furiously. "Oh! No, that's okay. I'm not much of a dancer."

Hayden had been watching India intently, and now she leaned forward, her smooth brow furrowed with concentration. "You know, something's been bugging me since we met the other night at Dylan's house. There's something about you that seems so familiar, but I can't put my finger on it. I could swear I've either seen you before, or we've met before."

"Oh, I don't think that's possible," India said.

"Hmm. I'm not sure." Hayden narrowed her gaze on the

other woman. "I can't put my finger on it, but it will come to me."

"You know what?" India said brightly, as she grabbed Lucas by the hand. "On second thought, I think I would like to dance!"

Before he could protest, she had pulled him onto the small dance floor, and moved easily into his arms as if it was the most natural thing in the world. The music switched to a slow, throbbing love song, and several other couples joined them on the small floor.

Lucas liked the way India felt in his arms as he drew her slowly around the floor. His cheek pressed against her hair, and the citrusy scent of her shampoo filled his senses.

"Why the sudden change of heart?" he asked quietly in her ear.

She pulled back just enough to look at him, and Lucas almost lost his step, gazing into her eyes. "I just thought it would be nice. Something else I haven't done."

"Dance?" he asked, skeptical.

"No. Country dance. They don't dance like this back east."

Lucas drew her closer, shifting his hand so that it settled at the small of her back, while he curled his other hand around her fingers. She fit perfectly against his big frame, soft where he was hard, and slim where he was bulky with muscle.

"Have you met Hayden before?" he asked.

She shook her head, perfuming the air with her shampoo. "Not that I'm aware. Maybe I just have one of those faces."

Now it was Lucas's turn to pull back and look at her. "Trust me," he said, his voice rich with sincerity. "You do not have *one of those faces*. I doubt anyone, having met you once, would forget your face."

He punctuated his words with a single stroke of his thumb along her cheek. He knew exactly why she had dragged him onto the dance floor; she'd been worried that Hayden might figure out who she was and spill the beans to him and Dylan. Maybe she'd already figured it out, and was just waiting for India to return to the table before she broke the news. Lucas hoped not. For reasons of her own, India clearly didn't want anyone to know her identity. If Hayden discovered who she was, Lucas knew India would disappear again. Suddenly, it became important to keep her close.

India stared at him now, searching his eyes, and then drew his head down to press a soft kiss against his mouth. Her lips were as soft and lush as he remembered from the previous night, and it took all his willpower to not stop in the middle of the dance floor and kiss her the way he ached to. As it was, he made a misstep and almost stumbled. India broke the luscious contact, and with a small sound of embarrassment, moved deeper into his arms as the dance ended.

"Remind me not to kiss you when I'm doing something

dangerous," he said, smiling against her temple. "Like dancing."

She giggled, and then pulled away and strove to look dignified as they made their way back to the table. Dylan tried and failed not to contain his knowing grin, but Lucas ignored him.

"So, the Harvest Fest starts tomorrow," Hayden said, leaning toward India. "I'll be working one of the booths, but you two should definitely come downtown and check it out! Bring your sister—I'm sure she would love it."

Their food arrived, and they waited while the waitress passed around plates and refilled drink orders.

"We'll have a booth set up down near the lake," Dylan added. "We're renting kayaks and paddleboards, and we'll be raffling off some adventures."

"That sounds like fun," India enthused, and glanced at Lucas. "I wouldn't mind renting a kayak."

Lucas couldn't prevent a swell of pleasure when she looked at him, as if it was a foregone conclusion that they would go to the festival together.

"Whatever you'd like," he agreed smoothly. "I've never attended the Harvest Fest, so this will be fun for me, too."

"You're in for a treat," Hayden said, smiling. "I'm looking forward to the farmer's market, with all the locally grown produce."

"Laurel is entering the pumpkin pie baking contest," Dylan said, as he took a hefty swallow of beer. "She won the contest last year, but she said the recipe she's using this year is even better."

Lucas rubbed his palms together. "I wonder if they need an extra tasting judge? I have a weakness for pumpkin pie."

The conversation was lighthearted and friendly, and Lucas found himself watching India with way too much interest. He loved the play of emotions across her face, her quick laugh, and her quicker wit. She'd apparently decided Dylan was a friend, because she didn't spare him her friendly jibes any more than she did Lucas. He also noticed how her glance returned to him again and again over the course of the evening, and at least once he found her watching him when she thought he wasn't looking. Before Lucas realized, three hours had passed.

"I should get going," India said, glancing apologetically at Lucas. "I don't want my mother to worry."

"I'll take you home," he offered immediately, pushing down his disappointment at seeing the day draw to a close.

They said their good-byes and made their way outside to Lucas's Jeep. The air had turned cold and crisp, and he didn't miss how India shivered as they made their way across the parking lot. Opening the back of the Jeep, he pulled out a fleece jacket he had stashed there earlier and draped it over her shoulders.

"I'll get the heat going. You'll be warm in just a minute."

Inside the Jeep, he cranked the heat and reached across India to adjust the vents. His hand brushed her leg, and he didn't miss her swiftly indrawn breath. He stilled, his arm stretched across the space between them.

"India," he breathed.

They stared at each other across the dark interior of the Jeep, and afterward Lucas couldn't have said who moved first. All he knew was that she was finally where he'd needed her to be the entire day, in his arms.

Chapter Ten

THE KISS WAS urgent and hot, so hot and sweet that India couldn't prevent the moan that slipped from her lips, any more than she could prevent her hands from gripping the hard bulk of his shoulders to pull him closer.

He tasted faintly of beer and something minty, and as his tongue invaded her mouth, she shivered with pleasure. Lucas made a low, rumbling sound of approval in his throat, and one big hand came up and angled her head for better access.

This.

This is what she had been craving. This is what she had been missing her entire life, even before the accident.

Her fingers curled into the hard muscle between his neck and shoulder. When she felt his hand slide along her rib cage and cup her breast through her blouse, she arched involuntarily into the heated caress. His fingers were skillful, kneading the pliant flesh and then finding her nipple and teasing it to a tight, aching bud.

"I need to see you," he muttered against her lips.

They broke apart, and India collapsed back against the seat, panting. She watched through hazy eyes as he unbuttoned the front of her blouse. He looked up at her, his eyes gleaming by the indistinct light of the dashboard. Cool air wafted over her bare skin as he parted the material, button by button, until finally only the fragile barrier of her white, lace bra separated her skin from his questing fingertips.

"Baby, you are so pretty," he breathed softly, and stroked a fingertip over the gentle swell of her breast above the lacy cup.

His fingers were callused, and India felt the scrape of roughness across her flesh like the rasp of a kitten's tongue. She shivered. He cupped her breast and brushed a thumb over her nipple, before he tugged the material downward and drew the sensitive peak into his mouth. India's breath escaped on a low moan, and her hands moved to his head to hold him there, her fingers threading through the warm layers of his hair. He laved her breast with his tongue and mouth, and India shifted restlessly on the seat. When Lucas slid a hand between her legs and cupped her intimately, pressing his thumb against the seam of her jeans, she reacted instinctively, rising to meet the exquisite pressure.

"India, sweetheart," he said, releasing her breast. "Come back to the inn with me. I want you so much, but let's do this right. It's been years since I've had sex in a car, and I'm out of practice."

India stared at him, her brain hazy with pleasure and her own rising need. She'd be lying to herself if she said she didn't want him, too. With his hand still warm between her thighs, and her breasts still tingling from his attention, she couldn't think of anything she wanted more than Lucas Talbot.

"Okay," she heard herself say.

"Is that a yes?" His voice was rough, cautiously hopeful.

India knew she was making a huge mistake. She had no business getting involved with Lucas Talbot, but suddenly she didn't care. Her future was uncertain. Why shouldn't she grab whatever happiness she could, while she could? Lucas was a decent man who made her want to do indecent things with him.

"That's a yes," she confirmed in a whisper. "Just...drive fast."

Lucas gave her a tender smile and swiftly adjusted her clothing, buttoning her blouse before he pulled the seat belt across her body and buckled her in.

"Call your mother and let her know you're okay," he said.

India nodded, and retrieved her phone. She couldn't bring herself to call, so took the coward's way out and sent a message to both her mother and her sister.

Staying out late with friends. Don't worry and don't wait up.

Within seconds, she received a response from her sister.

Where R U? U OK?

She punched in a swift reply. *Never better. Go to bed.*

"Everything okay?" Lucas asked, glancing at her phone.

"Yes."

"You are not going to regret this," he promised her, as he thrust the Jeep into gear.

He kept her hand in his as he navigated the roads that brought them to the Snapdragon Inn, rubbing his thumb across her palm. India watched him, admiring his strong profile, recalling the pressure of his mouth against hers. Soon they were pulling into the parking lot behind the inn, and Lucas came around to help her out.

"What if someone sees us?" she asked.

"We'll go in through the back," he said. "There's a staircase that leads almost to my room. Most of the other guests are either in bed, or down by the lake enjoying the fire pit."

India let him lead her to a back entrance and followed him along an extravagantly paneled hallway to a narrow staircase lit with small wall sconces. On the second floor, they turned left down a wide corridor, before Lucas stopped in front of a door and inserted a key. He opened the door for her, and then stepped in after her, closing and locking it behind them.

A small light had been left on beside the enormous king-size bed, and India had a vague impression of a richly furnished suite with a fireplace and separate sitting area, and French doors that led to a private balcony.

Lucas stood with his shoulder leaning against the door-frame, watching her as she surveyed her surroundings. His suitcase had been stashed in a corner, and a laptop sat closed on a small desk near the windows. On the other side of the bed, a door led to the bathroom, and everything had been done in rich shades of gold and navy blue. The bedside light provided enough illumination that they wouldn't stumble into furniture, but cast most of the room in deep shadows.

"Pretty room," India murmured, and cast a quick glance at him.

He pushed away from the door, and walked toward her, his movements as graceful and tightly coiled as a big cat's. He stopped in front of her.

"Changed your mind?" he asked softly.

India searched his face. His green eyes were intense, and a muscle worked in his lean jaw.

"No," she said, but took a tentative step backward, until she bumped against the bed.

Studying her the way an artist would a blank canvas, Lucas reached out and brushed a stray curl from her temple, before stroking the back of his fingers along the side of her face, and down the length of her neck. Up close, India could see the fine lines that radiated from the corners of his eyes, as well as the thickness of his lashes. A small scar bisected one eyebrow, and she wondered if he had once sported a piercing there. A growth of beard shadowed his jaw, darker at the spot where his chin bore a slight cleft. Her gaze dropped lower, to his mouth, and her breath hitched.

"Jesus, you are so sweet to look at," he murmured. His hands still rested on her shoulders, and now he urged her forward, into his arms.

India went willingly, tipping her face up as her eyelids fluttered closed. But whatever she had expected, it wasn't the slow, searching exploration of her mouth. He coaxed her lips apart, and then feasted on her, his tongue a slow, hot slide against her own. India gave a soft moan and angled her head to give him better access.

She felt his fingers working the buttons on her blouse, and without breaking the kiss, she began tugging at the hem of his jersey, pushing it upward until her hands encountered the hot satin of his skin. Lucas succeeded in unbuttoning her blouse and pushed it off her shoulders until she could shake it free from her arms. He immediately went to work on the fastening of her bra, releasing the clasp in one deft movement. When India would have pressed closer, he broke the kiss and stepped back, taking her bra with him. His eyes swept over her, and India didn't have time to feel self-conscious.

"Jesus, baby, you are fucking gorgeous," Lucas said, with feeling. Reaching over his head, he fisted one hand in the material of his shirt and dragged it over his head.

India forgot to breathe.

The guy was so incredibly hard and ripped, it hurt to look at him. India had known he was layered with muscles, but she hadn't guessed he would be so sleek and powerfully built. His pecs were firm and rounded, his abdomen a perfect washboard of muscle. A light sprinkling of dark hair covered his chest, before it traced its way downward and disappeared beneath the waistband of his jeans.

Without conscious thought, India closed the distance between them, and placed a hand in the center of his chest. Beneath her palm, she could feel the hard, heavy throb of his heart, and it caused an answering pulse between her legs. Lucas's eyes never left hers, but at the first touch of her hand against his skin, he gave a low groan, and then he was hauling her against all that firmness, and his tongue invaded her mouth as he kissed her with a sweet, hot urgency. India's breasts flattened against his chest, and her hands went to his back to slide over the long muscles along his spine and press him even closer.

Before she could protest, he lifted her in his arms and then deposited her on the bed, following her with the length of his body. He came over her, bracing himself on one elbow as he slid his free hand over her skin. He cupped one breast and then dipped his head to suck the tight peak into his mouth. India gasped at the sensation of heat and wetness, and felt an answering rush of moisture at her center. God, he felt so good! She tunneled her fingers through his hair, arching beneath his hot, talented mouth. But it wasn't enough.

"I want to see you," she implored, and reached for the buckle on his belt. She fumbled for a moment, until he brushed her hands aside and unfastened first the buckle and then the button on his jeans with fingers that trembled.

"Hold on a sec," he said, and stood up, pulling off her sneakers and socks, and then unfastening the button on her jeans, and working them down over her legs. India helped him, lifting her hips and kicking the pants free. She had no time to feel self-conscious as he swiftly shucked his clothing, and then he was gloriously, heart-stoppingly naked. Every inch of his body was hard, unadulterated male.

India's mouth went dry at the sight of his erection, and she opened her arms wide as he came back over her. He slid his arms beneath her and hefted her more fully into the center of the mattress. India laughed, touching him everywhere, as she pressed frantic kisses against his face and neck.

"Tell me what you want," he said, pulling her onto her side to face him, and lifting one leg over his hip.

"You, just you."

"You've got me, baby." His hands began a slow, thorough exploration of her body, and everywhere his fingers roamed, he followed with his mouth and tongue, until India was reduced to a quivering mass of aching nerve endings. She burned for him, every cell in her body crying out for fulfillment. Twice, he brought her to the edge of release with his clever fingers, but stopped just short of allowing her to plummet over the edge.

"Lucas, please—"

"Soon, sweetheart."

She could feel him, hot and hard, pressing against her stomach. Reaching between their bodies, she found him and wrapped her hand around his straining length, both thrilled and impressed by his heat and size. But when she stroked him, he gave an audible groan and turned her onto her back, grasping both her hands and holding them over her head.

"Easy, baby," he said, and his voice was a rough rasp in her ear. "I won't last if you do that."

"I want you inside me," she managed to say, catching his face and kissing him deeply.

Leaning over the side of the bed, he grabbed his jeans and shook them until his wallet fell out of the back pocket. India watched as he retrieved a foil packet and tore it open with his teeth, before sheathing himself. India opened for him, wanting him desperately, and then he was there, pressing into her with long, sure strokes.

India gasped, and her entire body clenched around him. She wanted to remember this moment; imprint it on her memory so that she would never forget the look and feel of Lucas Talbot as he claimed her. She drew her knees back, locking her ankles around his hips as he surged into her, gripping the big muscles of his shoulders with her fingers. He stared down at her, his eyes brilliant green in his flushed face.

"Jesus, India," he panted, his skin damp beneath her palms. "You're so snug."

"Harder," she begged, her voice a breathy pant. "I'm so close."

Reaching between their bodies, his fingers found the

most sensitive part of her. He swirled his thumb over her, and she was lost as an orgasm pounded over her, long and powerful. With a broken cry, she contracted hard and tight around him, her entire body bowing off the bed. Only then did Lucas slide his hands beneath her buttocks, tilting her hips upward as he drove into her, harder and deeper, his cock a thick, hot glide inside her pulsing flesh until finally, he gave a strangled cry and came in a series of shudders, before he collapsed over her.

IT WAS AFTER midnight when Lucas dropped her off at her house, walking her to the front door where the lights had been left on.

"Thank you," she said, turning to him. "I had a really great time tonight—today—all day."

"I wish you'd stay with me at the inn tonight," he said quietly, and slid a hand to her jaw, his fingers warm against her skin.

India looked at him, marveling again that his man wanted her. He was so big and vital and handsome, and her heart twisted with the knowledge that whatever they had found together was only transient.

"Believe me, there's nothing I want more, but my mother wouldn't understand," she finally said, although she wondered if that was true. Her mother would want India to do exactly as she pleased.

Bending his head down, Lucas pressed a kiss against her mouth, his lips warm and firm as they moved over hers. Within seconds, India felt a traitorous lick of desire, and gently pushed him away.

"If you keep that up, I'm going to end up dragging you inside and into my bed," she teased him.

"Spend tomorrow with me," he urged softly, and bent his head to hers. "I want to be with you. We can see the festival, and maybe sneak away for a few hours."

India knew she should put some space between them. She should tell him she had plans to go to the festival with her sister and mother. She'd already risked so much.

"Yes," she heard herself say. "I'll spend the day with you tomorrow."

He kissed her again, a long, slow mating of their mouths and tongues, until he set her aside with a rueful laugh.

"Okay, I should go now. Good night, baby."

India watched him walk to his Jeep, and only when the taillights had vanished, did she let herself into the house. Almost immediately, Katie materialized from the shadows.

"India!" she hissed. "Where have you been?"

"With Lucas."

Katie followed India into her bedroom, and waited while India turned on the light. India didn't miss how Katie's eyes widened.

"Oh my God," Katie breathed, and covered her mouth

with her hands, her eyes round as lollipops. "You slept with him!"

"I did, yes." India sat down on the edge of the bed. "Is it that obvious?"

"You're all pink, and your mouth is swollen," she observed.

Katie walked forward and sat down beside India, and the mattress sagged beneath their combined weight. India toed her sneakers off, unwilling to meet her younger sister's eyes.

"How was it?"

India did look at her then, letting the honesty of her words show on her face. "The most sublime experience I have ever had. I like him so much, Katie. We're spending tomorrow together."

"Oh, India." Katie's smooth brow furrowed. "Does he know?"

India didn't pretend to misunderstand. She shook her head.

"Are you going to tell him?"

How, exactly, did you tell the man you'd just slept with that your life expectancy was uncertain? India didn't want Lucas treating her any differently than he'd done today. She didn't want his pity, didn't want him treating her with kid gloves. For all she knew, her medical condition could be a deal breaker for him. If that was the case, she'd rather not know. She just wanted to hold on to whatever this was between them, for however long she could.

"No. I can't tell him," she said. "It would ruin everything."

Katie made a sympathetic sound, and put a hand on India's back, gently rubbing between her shoulder blades. "Do you think you will?"

Lifting her head, she searched Katie's eyes. "How can I? I'll only end up hurting him."

"You'll do that anyway," Katie said quietly. "Especially if you don't tell him."

Chapter Eleven

INDIA HAD PROMISED to meet Lucas by the entrance to the wide pier that extended out over the lake, at noon. Now he leaned negligently against the railing, enjoying the warmth of the sun on his shoulders, and the sound of laughter and conversation around him.

The Harvest Fest was bigger than he'd anticipated, with dozens of vendors hawking a rich diversity of arts and crafts, fresh produce, mums, pumpkins, baked goods, and the final offerings of farmer's market produce. His stomach rumbled as he smelled the aromas of food-truck fare like roasted nuts, steak sandwiches, and kettle corn. Live entertainment included fiddlers and dancers performing under the gazebo, and a large tent had been erected near the water, where the pumpkin pie baking contest would be judged later that day.

Shading his eyes, Lucas looked along the shoreline to where Jamie and Dylan had a tent set up by the water. He could see the kayak trailer nearby, and a line of paddleboards leaning against a display. Already, the lake was dotted with bright red, yellow, and green kayaks, and he watched as a young couple rented two paddleboards, and carefully pushed themselves away from the beach, and toward the deeper water of the lake.

"Hey, there you are! Have you been waiting long?"

Lucas turned sharply, and there she was. If possible, India looked even prettier today than she had yesterday, in a turquoise blouse that complemented her olive skin tone. She wore a flowing white skirt and sandals, and silver disk earrings dangled from her earlobes, catching the sunlight. A wide-brimmed, straw hat covered her dark curls, and her eyes were hidden behind a pair of sunglasses.

"Hey," he said warmly, and straightened from the railing to lean over and kiss her warmly.

"Um, Lucas, you've met my mother, Joanna Sullivan."

For the first time, Lucas realized India wasn't alone. Her mother and sister lingered behind her, and now the older woman stepped forward. Despite the smile on her face, Lucas didn't miss the sharply assessing eyes.

"Mrs. Sullivan," he said, and extended his hand. "It's nice to see you again."

"You can call me Joanna," she said, placing her hand in his.

He hadn't looked closely at her the night he'd fixed the electrical issue at the Howden house, but knew Joanna was fifty-four, just a few years younger than his own mother. While she was slender and attractive, the signs of her age were evident in the fine lines around her eyes and mouth, and the strands of silver at her temples. Her gray eyes considered him for a moment.

"So, you're from North Carolina?" she finally asked.

"Not originally," he said easily. "I moved there after I joined the military, since that's where my unit was located."

"A soldier, hmm? So not an electrician." A smile teased her mouth.

"A former soldier," he corrected her. "I got out a couple of months ago."

"What brings you to Glacier Creek?" she asked now, tipping her chin up as she watched him. "You're a long way from home."

"Mom," India protested. She gave Lucas an apologetic smile. "You don't need to ask why he's here, when the answer is obvious. Just look around us! Lake, mountains, fresh air…why wouldn't he come here?"

"It's okay," Lucas said. "I used to come here with my family when I was a kid. I've always loved Glacier Creek. What about you? How did you discover this place?"

Joanna stared at him, momentarily at a loss for words, but Lucas didn't miss how her gaze flicked to India. Then she hastily hitched her pocketbook higher on her shoulder and smiled. "Enjoy yourselves today. It was nice seeing you again, Lucas."

India came to stand beside him as they watched Katie and her mother walk in the direction of the farmer's market. When he finally looked at India, she pulled a face.

"I'm so sorry," she said. "My mom is a little overprotective since my accident. She wants me to enjoy myself, but she doesn't want to let me out of her sight. I try to cut her some slack, but I had no idea she'd be so—"

"It's okay," Lucas assured her. "Come here."

He caught her hand and tugged her into his arms. Carefully, he removed her sunglasses. She gazed up at him, and what he saw in her eyes made his breath catch. He tipped her hat back and lowered his mouth over hers. She tasted like sweet mint, and her body settled against his as if it was the most natural thing in the world. He kissed her for several long moments, until he became aware they were drawing amused glances from pedestrians.

Reluctantly, he pulled away, and handed her the sunglasses. "Sorry," he muttered. "I've been thinking about doing that since I said good night to you."

In fact, Lucas hadn't gotten any sleep after he'd dropped India off the night before. He'd spent the entire night replaying what had happened, over and over again in his head. But thinking about her had only aroused him again, until finally he'd gotten dressed and gone for a long, hard run along the lake. The physical exertion had felt good, but it hadn't stopped him from thinking about India.

He was in serious trouble.

He should come clean, tell her the truth about who he was, and ask her about her relationship with Martin Howden. Lucas didn't consider himself a coward, but just thinking about what that would do to India scared the shit out of him.

She would despise him for his duplicity, and he wouldn't blame her.

"Hey," she said now, pulling his arm around her waist as they strolled to the end of the pier. "You look very serious right now. Penny for your thoughts?"

"I was just thinking how lucky I am," he said.

"I'm the lucky one," she protested. "Never in a million years did I think I'd find someone like you, here in Montana. I came here to—"

She broke abruptly off, and when Lucas glanced at her, her mouth had compressed to a flat line.

"What did you come here for, India?" he asked.

She lifted one shoulder. "I don't know. To forget, maybe."

Reluctant to ruin the day, Lucas didn't press her. Instead, he gave her a squeeze and drew her down onto one of the benches that had been built into the side of the railing.

"For today," he said, squinting into the bright sunlight, "I want you to forget everything except having fun, okay? Where do you want to start?"

India smiled at him, uncertain. "Well, I am pretty hungry, and I did promise Hayden we would stop by her booth to say hello. Then I thought maybe we could rent some kayaks and go for a paddle?"

"Food it is," he said, and pulled her to her feet. "I spotted the perfect place on my way in, earlier."

With India tucked against his side, they meandered their way through the festival until they arrived at a food tent with long tables and benches set up in the shade. While India saved their seats at one table, Lucas snagged them a tray of food.

"What is this?" India asked when he returned, throwing a leg over the bench to sit beside her.

"This just happens to be one of the best steak sandwiches you've ever tasted," he promised. "Made from grass-fed Montana beef. You're in for a treat."

Thick, juicy slabs of steak, dripping with garlic butter, inside a crusty hunk of bread and served with a tall lemonade, seemed like a perfect way to start the afternoon. India carefully lifted her sandwich from the plate and eyed it doubtfully.

"It's so big."

"That's what she said," Lucas quipped, and winked at her.

As he'd hoped she would, she laughed.

"Okay, I'm going in," she said, and took a healthy bite, before closing her eyes and chewing in bliss. "Oh, oh, this is so good!"

From where they sat, they could hear the fiddlers and watch people strolling past. After they finished their sandwiches, they each had a second lemonade, before they made their way back into the stream of foot traffic. Lucas kept his arm protectively around India to prevent her from getting jostled by those walking in the opposite direction. Lucas knew India was feeling relaxed and he was glad. He preferred that to the seriousness of her earlier mood. For now, she seemed content to hang on to his arm, and let him lead her from booth to booth.

They found Hayden beneath a bright tent, carefully painting colorful designs on the faces of children and adults alike. She smiled and waved, but Lucas could see she was too busy to take a break.

"Oh, I want to see the jewelry at this next booth," India said, and pulled him behind her. "Look, these bracelets remind me of the ones we were looking at that first day in the shop." She looked at him for confirmation. "Do you remember?"

Lucas did. That first day in Glacier Creek seemed like an eternity ago. Had it really been just five days ago? So much had happened in the interim, and he no longer felt like the same man. He realized he had no interest in dredging up the past or learning what India's relationship had been with Martin Howden. In fact, he would call Meredith tonight and tell her the deal was off. He would no longer be her spy.

"I do remember," he said now, forcing himself to smile at her. "You didn't much like me. You practically dragged your sister out of the shop."

"I didn't *trust* you," she corrected him, as she inspected a pair of earrings. Without looking at him, she gently bumped against him with her hip. "I didn't know you then, like I do

144

now."

She didn't know him now, either. And she shouldn't trust him. The knowledge of his own deception made him feel a little ill. "Let me get the earrings for you," he said, taking the tiny hoops from her fingers. "These will look pretty on you."

"You don't have to buy them for me," she protested. "I have my own money."

Fifty million, to be exact. Yeah, he knew. And suddenly he no longer cared. "Let me," he said. "Don't you know it makes a guy feel good to buy something for his girl?"

As the sales girl took his money and turned away to slip the earrings into a small bag, India looked at him. "Is that what I am? Your girl?"

Her voice was teasing, but Lucas didn't miss the underlying seriousness in her tone.

"What do you think?" he asked, as he handed her the small bag.

"I think you're very mysterious," she said, studying him. "Do you really have twin sisters?"

"I do."

"Will I get to meet them someday?"

"Someday, sure. I don't see them very often myself."

"Where do they live?"

Lucas hesitated. He didn't want to tell her they lived in the Hamptons, just outside of New York City. Unless he was careful, he could inadvertently give her too much information. It wouldn't be hard to put two and two together and figure out who he really was. A part of him was surprised she hadn't already figured it out.

"My mom has a place in California," he finally said, giving her a partial truth. "They live with her there when they're not in college. C'mon, let's go rent a couple of kayaks."

The rental tent was busy, with nearly every paddleboard and kayak already rented out. Only one kayak remained, and it was only a single-seater.

"I wish you'd said something," Dylan said with a frown. "I'd have set two kayaks aside for your use."

"Hey, we just had two come back in," Jamie said, walking up from the shore. "They're all yours!"

Lucas helped India secure her life vest, and then held her kayak steady as she lowered herself into the seat.

"I'll give you a push out onto the water," he said. "Ready?"

India gave a little squeal as the kayak rocked, and then she was gliding over the water, using her paddle to adjust her direction. Satisfied she wasn't about to tip herself into the lake, Lucas jumped into his own kayak and set out after her.

"Where shall we go?" she asked. "I'm not familiar with the lake."

"Let's head south," he suggested. "There are some pretty bays, and we'll stay close to shore."

He let India lead the way, admiring her efficient use of the paddle as she stroked the oars through the water. Soon they left the festival and the town behind. Although he could no longer see the pier or the festival, he could still hear strains of music from the band, amplified by the speakers over the water. He lengthened the stroke of his oars and glided up next to India's kayak.

"What do you think?" he asked.

"It's beautiful." She rested the oar across her lap and leaned back in her seat. "I used to do sea-kayaking, as a kid. We lived right on the ocean. But this is much different, much more relaxed."

They drifted beneath the overhanging limbs of a tree, and Lucas maneuvered his kayak so that he could lift several branches out of her way. They disturbed a pair of loons, who flapped their wings furiously against the water in their haste to escape.

"Gorgeous," India commented, watching them land further out on the water, where the sun made the surface sparkle. She lifted a hand, pointing to the surrounding mountains. "Look, you can see the colors beginning to change. It's going to happen fast now that the nights have grown cold."

Following her finger, Lucas could indeed see the autumn colors of gold and russet starting to dominate the landscape. During the time he'd spent in Yemen, he'd missed winter and its bright, cold embrace, but not nearly as much as he'd missed the brilliant change of season that characterized the Hudson River valley and New York in autumn.

They continued to drift, lazily steering the kayaks through the water, until they rounded an outcropping of land and entered a small, private bay. Situated on a knoll overlooking the water, stood the Snapdragon Inn. The view from the lake was spectacular, and Lucas realized from this vantage you could see the magnificent, round turret that dominated one side of the structure, and the equally impressive, rounded terrace that extended off the back of the house.

"Hey, is this where you're staying?" India asked.

"It is."

"I didn't realize just how big—and beautiful—it is! Look at that lawn, sweeping right down to the edge of the water, and that amazing patio!" She peered closer. "Is that your room, on the second floor, with the balcony?"

"That's it," he confirmed.

She gave him a look that clearly said she was impressed. "How'd you manage to score such a prime view?"

Lucas laughed. "I didn't ask for anything special, if that's what you're implying. Maybe that's all they had left."

"I know, I know," she said with an exaggerated sigh. "The Howden mansion was already booked."

"Why don't we bring the kayaks in, and I'll see if Mia can whip us up something to drink."

"Mm, that sounds good," she agreed, and they steered the kayaks toward shore.

There were no guests lingering by the water today, nor did they encounter anyone as they made their way across the sweeping lawn to the house.

"Maybe everyone has gone into town for the festival," India said.

"It certainly seems so," Lucas agreed.

Taking India's hand, they climbed the stone steps to the large, curved patio that overlooked the lake. Cozy groupings of Adirondack chairs and tables made it easy to see why guests would want to linger here, especially as the sun began to set in the west.

Lucas used his key card to access the door to the dining room, and he heard India's delighted gasp as she took in her surroundings.

"Wow, this place is unbelievable," she said. "Look at the woodwork, and the details! Somebody put a lot of money and heart into restoring this place."

"Yeah, that would be Mia Davies," Lucas said. "She said she purchased the place when it was up for auction. She actually saved it from being torn down."

"I'm sure some big developer is crying into his beer that he lost that opportunity," she observed.

"No doubt."

They made their way through the inn to the kitchen, where they startled an older woman who was rolling out pastry on the enormous pastry board.

"Oh!" she said, clapping a hand to her heart. "You gave me a start! I thought all the guests had gone into town for the festival."

"We were just there," Lucas said. "But we rented some kayaks and somehow ended up here. Is it okay I left them pulled up on the lawn?"

"Of course." She brushed her hands on the front of her apron. "I'm Mia's mother, Dot. I used to own the Gingersnap Bakery in town, before I decided to retire and help out with the inn." She gestured toward the dough on the counter. "Now I just bake for the guests. I'm making cinnamon buns, for the morning."

Lucas extended his hand. "I'm Lucas Talbot—I'm staying here—and this is my friend, India Cordoza. We were actually just looking for something to drink and then we'll get out of your way."

"Oh, my dears, you're not in the way. The fridge is over there; just help yourself to whatever strikes your fancy. There's beer and wine, and we have a fully stocked bar in the library if you'd like something stronger."

Lucas grinned at India. "I think water or lemonade will be perfect." He opened the fridge and peered inside. "Where is Mia today?"

"She went into town with friends. They were planning to have lunch there and do some shopping. Nice for her to get away every now and then."

Lucas selected several cold drinks from the fridge. "Thanks, Dot."

Taking India's hand, he pulled her back through the house, and up the main staircase.

"Where are we going?" India whispered loudly.

Lucas paused on the first landing of the staircase, where an enormous stained glass window cast fractured beams of colored light over their faces.

"Is this okay?" he asked. "I've been thinking all day about how I can get you back in my bed."

"Better than okay," she assured him, and slid her arms around his waist, pressing close enough that he felt the softness of her breasts flatten against his chest. "I'm just glad I'm not the only one who's been thinking about getting naked all day."

Truth be damned. Lucas knew then he would do anything to keep her.

Chapter Twelve

N O SOONER WERE they in the room, than Lucas tossed the unopened drinks onto the bed, and then flattened India against the nearest wall with his body. Her hands were everywhere, under his shirt and around his back, stroking his skin while she kissed his face and jaw and neck. Her fingers unfastened the buttons on his shirt, brushing his skin as she exposed it.

Lucas was heady with it, couldn't keep his hands off her. He kissed her, his tongue invading her mouth and drinking her in. Reaching up, he snatched her straw hat from her head and gave it a toss, and then did the same with her sunglasses and pocketbook.

"I want you naked," he growled, looking at her pretty blue blouse and wondering how best to remove it without shredding it, which would have been the quickest way.

India complied, peeling the shirt over her head and unfastening her bra, and then dragging his shirt upward, too, until he discarded it. Then they were pressed together, skin against skin. India's body was cool and soft, but when he bent his head down and sucked one of her nipples into his mouth, it was already tight with arousal. Her breathing quickened as she speared her fingers through his hair.

Reaching down, Lucas dragged the hem of her skirt upward, his hand sliding along the length of her leg until he encountered the edge of her panties and dragged them down. India helped him, and then there was nothing between his questing fingers and her hot, satiny center.

"Oh, Lucas," she gasped, when his fingers found her, searching through the curls to the slippery folds beneath.

"Jesus, India." She was already wet for him. He slid a finger along her cleft, and then swirled it over the nub of her clit, gratified when she made a small keening sound of pleasure. Behind the zipper of his jeans, he was already hard, harder than he'd ever been. Then her hands were there, undoing the belt buckle and the fastening of his pants, and he was helping her shove both his jeans and his boxers down over his hips. Reaching beneath her, he lifted her against the wall, his hands filled with her sweet ass, as she spread her thighs wide for him.

With a grunt of effort, he positioned himself at her opening, and then thrust upward and buried himself inside her in one slick, wet glide. He kept her in place with the weight of his body and his arms beneath her hips as she rode him, clinging to his neck. The sensation of her, hot and tight and so fucking wet for him was almost his undoing. She used her thighs to leverage herself, squeezing his cock with her inner muscles. Lucas gritted his teeth so hard that his back teeth ached with the effort not to come.

"Lucas, we're not using protection," India gasped.

A part of him recognized that those words should have been a much better deterrent than they actually were. In reality, they did absolutely nothing to tamp down his rising lust. In one movement, he turned with India still clinging to him, and managed to shuffle-step over to the bed, where he leaned forward and laid her down across the mattress, sweeping the water bottles onto the floor. Only then did he allow himself to pull out of her body.

Lucas quickly kicked off his shoes and dragged his pants free from his legs, without ever taking his eyes from India. She had no idea how tempting she looked, with her white skirt bunched around her waist, and her slim feet still encased in sandals while the rest of her was naked. Her breasts heaved with her breathing, and she drew her knees together, denying him a view of her pretty pussy.

Swiftly, he dug through his wallet and retrieved a condom, rolling it over himself, and then leaning down to kiss India. She shifted restlessly against the cover, and Lucas took his time kissing her, while his hand slid between her legs. She moaned at the first touch of his fingers. Slowly, Lucas continued making his way down the length of her body, pausing to kiss and suckle each breast in turn, sweeping his tongue across the puckered nipples. He lingered over her navel, teasing the small indent and gently raking his teeth over the rise of her hip bones.

She was incredibly responsive, her fingers threading through his hair, and either tightening their hold or relaxing, depending on the intensity of her need. When he reached the apex of her thighs, he looked up to find her watching him through hazy eyes. Slowly, he drew her knees apart, and bent his head and placed his mouth over the most sensitive part of her, licking her with deep, soft sweeps of his tongue. India cried out, and her hands clutched at his head just before her hips rose off the bed and began circling. He smiled against her flesh, and then added his fingers, working her until an orgasm broke. He watched as wave after wave of pleasure washed over her, and her slender body arched upward.

He didn't give her time to recover, stroking into her in one thick, powerful glide and seeing her mouth open on a wordless *oh* of wonder. He was so close, that it took no more than a half dozen swift strokes before he found his own release. Afterward, they lay on the bed, limbs entwined, and dozed. The last thing Lucas thought before he drifted to sleep was that nothing had ever felt as good as India Gale in his arms.

When he woke up an hour later, the sun was still high. India lay watching him, and for a moment he just let his gaze drift over her face, memorizing the texture of her skin and the perfection of her eyebrows, the lush fullness of her mouth.

"You are so beautiful," he murmured, and rubbed his

thumb along her lower lip, before replacing it with his mouth.

The kiss was slow and sensual, and within minutes, Lucas found himself hard again. India pulled back and stared into his eyes.

"It's the same for me," she said softly. Reaching for him, she encircled his rigid length with her hand, slowly stroking him until his breath began to come in fitful gasps.

"I don't have another condom," he finally managed to say, pushing down his disappointment.

"I'm safe," she said, and released him long enough to show him her forearm. "I have a birth control implant, here. I had it done before my accident, but it's good for another year, at least."

Lucas didn't like to think about what that meant, or why she had felt the need for a long-term birth control method. "I was clean at my last medical exam," he heard himself say. "I haven't been with anyone since."

"Well, then," India said, and gave him a slow, sexy smile that dispelled any last reservations he might have had.

He watched as India rose on one elbow, and when she kissed him, he felt it all the way to his toes. Slowly, she rose to her knees on the bed, and then came over him, straddling his hips. Gripping him in her hand, and keeping her gaze locked with his, she lowered herself down, sliding over him until he was fully seated inside her.

"Good?" she asked, looking down at him.

Lucas found himself completely incapable of coherent speech. He could only nod mutely. The sight and feel of India, over him and surrounding him, rendered him utterly speechless. Then she began to move, and he stared, mesmerized, as her breasts bounced gently.

She leaned forward, placing a hand on the pillow on either side of his face, and he buried his fingers in her soft curls, drawing her down to kiss her as she continued to ride him. Her inner muscles clenched hard around him, and Lucas knew he wasn't going to last, but he didn't want to come without her. Sliding a hand to the spot where they were joined, he stroked her with his fingers, rewarded when she gasped and increased her pace.

"Good?" he asked, finding his voice.

"So…good!" she managed in a choked voice, just before she contracted around him.

Gripping her hips, Lucas surged upward, finding his own release in a blinding, white-hot rush of pleasure. Afterward, India collapsed against his chest, her breath damp and uneven against his neck. Lucas stroked her hair and smoothed his other hand down the length of her prone body.

"Am I alive?" she asked weakly against his neck.

Lucas laughed softly, and then gently slapped her bottom. "Let's take a shower, and then we can kayak back to town."

"No," she moaned, laughing with him. "I have no energy left to kayak anywhere."

"I'll call Dylan and have him come out and collect us and the kayaks," he assured her. "We don't need to paddle back."

India rolled onto her back beside him, and then sat up, swinging her bare legs over the side of the bed. Lucas found himself admiring the long, supple lines of her spine when something else made him look closer. Her back was covered with tiny white and pink splotches, almost like dozens of small starbursts. Frowning, he rose on one elbow and reached out to trace the markings with a fingertip. As soon as he did, India flinched, and then hastily stood up and turned to face him.

"I'll go turn the water on in the shower," she offered.

"India, your back—"

But she was already shaking her head. "It's nothing, Lucas, really."

But Lucas had been in the military for ten years. He'd seen his share of combat injuries, and he recognized the marks for what they were—shrapnel scars. Dozens and dozens of tiny scars from where her body had endured a barrage of flying material. He hadn't seen the scars last night, when the room had been in near darkness. Seeing them now disturbed him on a level so deep, he wasn't sure how to react.

He stood up and before she could retreat, he turned her toward the light from the window, studying the scars.

"Please, Lucas," she whispered in distress.

"Is this from the car accident?" But he already knew the

answer.

"I don't remember how I got out of the car," she said quietly. "But when it exploded, I was within the blast radius."

Lucas closed his eyes, feeling ill from the images his imagination conjured up in all too graphic detail. He'd read the police reports, had known the sports car had caught fire and then exploded, but he'd never really allowed himself to think about what that had meant for India Gale. She had survived the accident, but not without cost.

"I can see the sight of my scars upsets you," India said woodenly, pulling free. "I'll be sure to keep them covered in the future."

She turned to walk into the bathroom, her spine rigid, but Lucas caught her arm. "You're wrong," he said, bending his head down to look directly into her eyes. "Your scars do upset me, but not for the reasons you think."

"Why then?" Her dark eyes were wary as she watched him.

"I hate the thought of what you went through," he explained. "I've seen shrapnel scars before, India, many times. It would take more than that to make me turn away. But the idea of you in pain...that would keep me awake at night."

"I'm fine," she said, but she caught her lower lip between her teeth, and Lucas knew she was close to tears.

"C'mon," he said, and steered her toward the bathroom. "Let's take that shower and get dressed, and then we can talk."

Under the steaming spray of water, he soaped India's hair and skin, keeping his touch gentle and light. But as the water sluiced the soap suds from her back, he could see the scars clearly. Against her tawny skin, they stood out like handfuls of scattered stars. He found other scars, too, which he recognized as surgical scars. There was one at the nape of her neck, another near her buttock, and a third on the back of her thigh.

Finishing the shower, Lucas enfolded her in a wide, fluffy towel, and used a second one to absorb the moisture from her hair, which sprang around her face in wet curls.

Wrapping a third towel around his hips, he led her back into the bedroom.

"Do you want to tell me about the accident?" he asked quietly, as she walked to the windows and stood looking out at the lake.

"Not really," she murmured. "It was a year ago, and I feel like I'm finally moving past it. Talking about it will only revive all those old feelings again."

"I'd still like to hear what happened to you, India."

She bent her head down and sighed, and then turned to look at him. "Why is it so important for you to know?"

Lucas cocked his head and gave her a bewildered look. "You don't think I'd want to know about what you went through?"

She shrugged. "If you'd been injured during combat, do

you think you'd want to talk about it every time someone saw your scars? Does seeing them give someone the right to know how they were acquired?"

She had a point, but he'd hoped she trusted him enough to share her story—and her pain—with him.

"Okay, I get it and I won't press you," he said, reluctantly. "But just tell me you're okay now."

Crossing the room, she picked up her discarded clothes, began shaking them out and then started to get dressed.

"I'm fine, Lucas, really," she said, sliding her arms into her bra and fastening it. "The best thing you can do is just leave it alone."

But as they dressed, Lucas found himself thinking about those scars, and he knew he couldn't let it go. He'd find out what had happened that night, and then he'd figure out a way to make it right. He was beginning to realize that she may have lost more than he realized, and that fifty million dollars wasn't nearly enough compensation.

Chapter Thirteen

H E'D FALLEN FOR India Gale.
   Head over heels.

Lucas had never felt so certain, or so confused, about anything in his life. He'd come to Glacier Creek with the sole intention of spying on her, and had instead fallen in love with her.

He needed to come clean about who he was, but found he lacked the courage. He didn't believe she had slept with his stepfather; didn't think she was the type of woman to have an affair with a married man. Even if he was wrong about that, he told himself that whatever had happened before he met her was in her past. He was only interested in her future.

With him.

Not that they'd talked about that. He actually had no idea if India felt the same way about him, or not. But if her physical response to him was any indication, he thought he had a pretty good chance of persuading her to give their relationship a try.

His mother would be furious. She would try to punish

him, most likely by cutting him off financially, which would have absolutely no impact on his life. He hadn't required financial support of any kind since he'd left for college. Even his tuition had been paid for, since he'd received a full scholarship to West Point. She wouldn't be able to touch the inheritance his biological father left him, or even the small amount that Martin had left him. But money was the only thing Meredith Howden understood. The irony of the situation wasn't lost on Lucas.

He recalled again the scars he'd seen on India's smooth skin, and the haunted look in her eyes when he'd asked about them. There was no way he could go on without telling her the truth. He only hoped it wasn't too late.

In the end, they decided to paddle the kayaks back to the festival, where Dylan waited for them on the shore. As he helped Lucas pull the kayaks onto the beach, he gave Lucas a knowing look.

"I think you officially broke the record for the longest kayak rental today." He grinned broadly. "Did you have fun?"

India nodded, missing the exchange between the two men. "I loved every minute of it."

Lucas gave his friend a warning look. "Thanks for letting us use the kayaks."

They fist-bumped each other, and then Lucas tucked India's hand in his as they made their way back to Main Street, where the festival was still in full swing. The afternoon sun was beginning to dip behind the mountains, and the temperatures were starting to fall. Bright strings of colored lights hung across Main Street at regular intervals, and both the gazebo and the common that ran the entire length of Main Street had been festooned with bright outdoor bulbs.

"This is so pretty!" India exclaimed. "Look there, out on the lake!"

A parade of small sailboats drifted past, their sails outlined in colored lights as they made a brilliant, moving display across the lake.

"Beautiful," Lucas agreed, but his eyes were on India's face as she watched the procession of boats.

"India! Lucas!" They both turned at the sound of their names being called, to see Katie waving at them as she quickly made her way through the throngs of people. Her mother, Joanna, followed at a slower pace, but both women wore expressions of concern.

"India, I need to talk to you!" Katie said, breathless. "I have been looking for you everywhere. Where did you disappear to?"

"We rented some kayaks and took them out onto the lake," India said, sliding a look at Lucas. "We were gone longer than we planned."

"I wish you had told me first," Joanna said as she reached their side. "I was getting worried about you, especially when you didn't answer your phone."

"I'm sorry, Mom. I never heard it ring," India apologized. "Have you eaten? Why don't we get some food and go sit and listen to the band?"

They walked in the direction of the food tents, but Katie held India back. "I need to talk to you," she said in a low voice, but not so low that Lucas couldn't hear her.

Joanna tried to distract Lucas by drawing him into conversation, but he couldn't help overhear their hushed conversation.

"What is wrong with you?" India hissed. "You're both acting like mother hens! Can't I have any privacy?"

"It's not about that," Katie said, and her gaze flew to Lucas, who pretended to be absorbed in the story Joanna was telling him.

"Then what?" India asked.

"There was a reporter at the house today."

"What?" India blanched, and looked quickly at Lucas, before linking her arm with Katie's and bending her head down toward the younger woman. "What did he want?"

"It was a woman, and I didn't answer the door. She and her coworker hung around for a little bit before they finally left. But what if they're at the house when we return?"

"What did Mom think?" India asked.

"She doesn't know. I'd gone back to the house by myself because I'd forgotten my wallet. I didn't say anything to her because I didn't want to upset her. She'd probably make us leave Glacier Creek tonight, if she knew."

"We were so careful," India replied. "Robert said all the

records have been sealed, so there isn't anyone who knows I'm here. Not even the Howden family!"

Lucas glanced back at India, but she gave him a bright smile, as if she and her sister were discussing the weather. As they stopped in front of a vendor selling bowls of chili and homemade bread, Lucas considered what Katie had said. If a reporter had ventured out to the house, the visit could have been prompted by news that the house was going on the market, and not because India Gale was living there. The reporter could simply have been following up on that lead. Even something as mundane as the sale of Martin Howden's house could be enough to give the old story new life. Although he didn't like the thought of India selling the place, legally she could do what she wanted with the property.

He paid for the food and was carrying the tray over to a nearby table when Dylan approached.

"Hey, man," he said, eyeing the women. "I'm sorry to interrupt, but I was hoping you could give me a hand down at the lake. Jamie had to take off, and I could use some help getting the equipment back to the shop."

"Of course," Lucas said. "I'll be right there."

He was actually glad for the interruption. He found he had a difficult time keeping his hands to himself when she was around, but instinctively knew she wouldn't welcome any public displays of affection, at least not in front of her mother. He said his good-byes to the women, promising to call India later that evening. He was halfway to the lake when she caught up to him.

"Lucas, wait," she called, as she jogged to his side.

He paused. "Everything okay?"

She nodded. "Yes, but it doesn't feel right just letting you walk away, not after this afternoon."

Lucas understood. They had crossed a line in their relationship, had gone way past acquaintances or friends. But India hadn't seemed inclined to show any affection for him in front of her mother, so he had respected that. He hadn't tried to hold her hand or indicate by any word or gesture that they were romantically involved.

"I just assumed you would want to keep us under wraps," he said easily.

India hugged her arms around her middle and nodded, looking uncomfortable. "Not in the way you mean. My mother knows we're seeing each other, but she doesn't know that you and I—that we've—" She broke off, embarrassed. "My sister knows, but not my mother. I just don't want to give her a reason to worry about me. Thank you again for this afternoon. I had a really nice time."

"I had a great time, too. Listen, why don't I come by later and pick you up? We can go somewhere quiet and talk?"

India shook her head. "Thanks, but not tonight. I can feel a headache coming on, so I don't think I'd be very good company."

"Okay, I hope it's nothing serious?"

She shook her head. "Of course not. I'll get a good

night's sleep and be fine by tomorrow."

"Come out to the inn. We'll have lunch on the patio. I'll let Mia know."

"I'd like that." She gestured vaguely in the direction of the food tents. "Well…I should probably get back to my family. Good night, Lucas."

He stood for a moment and watched her walk away. Everything had changed since he'd first set out to find India Gale. He'd never meant to have feelings for her, and now he needed to tell her who he was. And that he was crazy about her.

He only hoped telling her the truth wouldn't drive her away forever.

INDIA WOKE UP with a start, disoriented and panicked. The room was completely dark, the only sound her labored breathing. It took her a minute to remember she was in the Glacier Creek mountain house. Pushing to a sitting position, she dragged a hand across her eyes, trying to dispel the nightmare. A fine sheen of sweat coated her skin, but the bedroom was cool. She shivered.

Reaching over, she switched on the bedside light. After a moment, the images that had pulled her, gasping, out of the nightmare, began to recede. Swinging her legs over the side of the bed, she pulled a soft throw from the foot and dragged it around her shoulders, welcoming the soft warmth. Walking across the room, she pushed the drapes aside and gazed with unseeing eyes out the window at the dark lake and distant mountains.

In her mind's eye, all she could see were flames. She heard again the sudden *whoosh* as the ruptured gas line ignited. She could smell the smoke, feel herself choking on the thick, acrid fumes. In her dream, she tried frantically to open the passenger door of the small sports car, but it refused to budge. In the last seconds before the flames shot out from under her seat and consumed her, she locked gazes with the driver.

Martin Howden.

In her dream, his mouth moved as he shouted indistinguishable words at her.

Then she woke up.

Knowing she wouldn't get back to sleep, she padded out to the kitchen and turned on the teakettle. When the water was hot, she poured herself a cup of Earl Gray and went into the great room to curl up on the sofa. She flicked on the television and finally settled on a comedy, although she couldn't concentrate enough to watch it.

"Hey, Sis, I thought I heard something. What are you doing up so early?"

India looked up to see Katie walk into the room, looking sleepy and disheveled in her oversized men's pajamas. India smiled at her, and patted the cushion next to her.

"I couldn't sleep. Come keep me company. Do you want a cup of tea?"

"No, thanks." Katie sat down next to India, tucking her feet up beneath her, and putting her head on India's shoulder. "Did you have another nightmare?"

India nodded. They'd been recurring with more frequency over the last few months, and they were usually the same. Tonight, though…this one had been different.

"I saw his face tonight."

"Whose face?"

"Martin Howden's. He was gesturing toward the driver's door, and he was trying to say something to me but I couldn't hear him."

Katie laced her fingers with India's. "You've never seen him before in your dreams."

"No. I'm always alone in the car, trapped, unable to escape. And then I burn."

Katie lifted her head, her expression distraught. "But you did escape. And now you're sitting here with me in this beautiful house."

"And Martin Howden is still dead."

"He was driving too fast—the police said so. The roads were wet, and he missed the curve. The accident had nothing to do with you, India."

India knew she was right. She'd read the police reports, and the accident investigation had concluded the driver had been operating the vehicle at an unsafe speed. When he realized he couldn't negotiate the curve in the road, he'd overcompensated, putting the car into a tailspin. The car had struck a utility pole while traveling backward, slicing through the rear bumper and igniting the gas tank. The force of the collision had warped the frame, making it impossible to open either the driver or the passenger doors. The investigators concluded the passenger window had shattered, allowing India to escape. Martin Howden never regained consciousness following the crash, and died in the explosion.

Now India passed a hand over her eyes. "You're right," she finally said. "But don't you see? This nightmare was different. This is the first time I've seen his face. I mean, I've obviously seen pictures of the man, but in my dream he seemed so real, as if I could literally reach out and touch him."

"Maybe your memories are beginning to return," Katie said. "Maybe the doctors were right, and you just needed to get away and allow yourself to relax and heal."

India nodded. While she wanted to believe Katie was right, she suspected the real reason her nightmares had become more vivid had to do with Lucas, and the fact he had seen her scars. Just remembering the tenderness with which he'd traced the markings on her back made her feel shivery inside. He'd said the scars didn't repel him, and she believed him. She knew what her doctor would say; by letting Lucas see the scars, she was accepting them. Once she accepted what had happened to her, the healing would begin.

"So, what's going on with you and Lucas?" Katie asked, bumping her shoulder against India's. "If I didn't know better, I'd say someone is in danger of falling in love."

"He's a really great guy," India acknowledged. "He's sweet and sexy, and I like being with him."

"But…?"

"But I can't let myself believe we have a future together. The house goes on the market next week. The property manager said he can handle the sale, but I think it's time we moved on. I'm going to donate the money from the house, maybe to a rehab center for traumatic brain injuries."

Katie frowned. "I thought we could stay through Christmas, at least."

"I don't know, Katie. The longer we stay here, the harder it's going to be to make a clean break."

"Then why are you sleeping with him, if you don't want a relationship with him?"

India turned to face her sister, surprised by the judgment she heard in Katie's voice.

"I never said I don't *want* a relationship with him," she protested. "I do, but I'm also realistic enough to know a long-term relationship isn't possible."

"No," Katie retorted, withdrawing her hand and pushing to her feet. "You don't know that. India, there are people all over the world living with uncertain futures. But they don't just put love on a shelf because they *might* die. You clearly like this guy, and I'm pretty sure he likes you. A lot. What you're doing isn't right."

"Don't judge me," India retorted, the words coming out sharper than she intended. "You don't know how you'd react until you're put in that position, and I hope to God something like this never happens to you."

"I'm sorry for what you're going through," Katie said, and swiped furiously at a tear. "But I think sleeping with a guy and letting him think there's something there, when there isn't, is just bullshit."

But there *was* something there. And that's why India needed to make a clean break. If she let things continue, she'd just end up with a broken heart.

"It's complicated," she finally said. "You don't know anything about it."

"Fine." Katie made a sweeping gesture with her arms. "I don't want to know. But I think if you just told him what's going on with you, you might be surprised. The guy cares about you!"

"I can't tell him," India insisted. "I've kept too much from him as it is. Besides, if I tell him the truth about everything and he decides to stay, I'll always wonder if it's me he wants, or the money."

"Oh, for Pete's sake," Katie groaned. "Does he look like he's in need of a loan? Why don't you start by telling him about your health issues, and see how he reacts? If he heads for the hills, then the money is a moot point."

Katie was right. Lucas Talbot seemed financially secure,

and his decision to remain in Glacier Creek to help run *Adrenaline Adventures* seemed driven by a sincere desire to be part of the business, and not by an empty wallet.

"Okay," she said reluctantly. "I'll tell Lucas about the shrapnel. You're right—if he can't handle that, then the rest won't matter."

"Tomorrow?" Katie persisted.

"I promise."

Leaning down, Katie gave her a hug. "You're doing the right thing," she said. "Lucas cares about you and he'll want to know the truth. He's a stand-up guy, Sis, and I know that when you tell him the truth, he'll stick by you."

As India watched her sister walk out of the room, she wished she felt as confident about Lucas's reaction.

Chapter Fourteen

INDIA WAS READY well before noon and found herself prowling restlessly. Now that she'd made the decision to tell Lucas everything about her identity, the injury, and the settlement, she just wanted to get it over with. Or avoid it altogether. She vacillated between conviction and self-doubt. Half a dozen times, she'd reached for the phone to call Lucas and cancel and had then changed her mind.

"Come sit down, sweetheart," her mother urged from the outside deck. "You're making me nervous with your pacing. You'd think this was your first date with Lucas!"

India felt like it was her first date. Despite the amazing sex she and Lucas had shared, nothing had ever made her feel as naked or vulnerable as the thought of sharing her limited life expectancy with him. She couldn't talk to her mother about it, though. If anyone was in denial about her prognosis, it was Joanna Sullivan. She spent most of her spare time researching new medical procedures and techniques, or making phone calls and sending emails to different surgeons, hoping to find someone who could safely remove the shrapnel.

When the doorbell rang, India jumped.

"I'll get it," she called, and drew in a deep, calming breath.

But when she opened the door, it was to see a young woman on the doorstep with a professional camera around her neck. A man stood behind her with a clipboard in his hand. Too late, India realized this must be the reporter her sister had seen yesterday.

"I'm sorry," she said quickly. "Whatever it is you're selling, we're not interested."

She tried to close the door, but the woman put her hand on the jamb. "We're here to do a quick walk-through of the house for the upcoming sale."

India paused. "You're not a reporter?"

The woman looked dumbfounded. "No, ma'am. I'm Kim and this is Devin. We work for Acker Property Management. I called and talked with Joanna Sullivan about coming by and looking at the house."

India opened the door wider, feeling foolish. "Of course. I'm so sorry. Please, come in."

The property management office had told her they would send someone by the house to take photographs, but they hadn't set a date or time. India had thought someone would call her first, and not just show up unannounced.

"Wow," Kim said, as she entered the house and stared around her in awe. "This is really stunning. If I had the money, I'd be tempted to buy this place myself."

"Mom?" India called. "There's someone here."

India's mother came in from the deck and gave India a questioning look.

"Mom, this is Kim and Devin from Acker Property Management. They're here to do a walk-through of the house for the sale. Did you know about this?"

"Ah," Joanna said with a smile. "Yes. They called your phone to set up the appointment, but you were sleeping and I didn't want to wake you up. After that, I completely forgot about it. I'm so sorry." She turned to Kim. "You said you wanted to do a walk-through to determine what kind of staging might be required for the photos? Come with me, I'll give you the tour and you can decide where to start."

As India gave her mother an exasperated but relieved smile, the doorbell sounded again. This time, Lucas stood at the entry, looking rugged and handsome in a pair of faded, worn jeans that hugged his strong thighs, paired with a T-shirt under a cotton, button-down shirt with the sleeves rolled back over his forearms.

"Hi," she said, and would have stepped outside and closed the door before he had a chance to peek inside, but she still needed to grab her pocketbook. Reluctantly, she opened the door and invited him in.

"Oh, Lucas," her mother said, beaming. "It's wonderful to see you again."

"Good morning, Joanna," he said, and his gaze moved to Kim and Devin, and the camera that hung around the woman's neck. Before India could make introductions, he extended a hand toward Kim. "I'm Lucas Talbot."

"I'm Kim Benatti, with Acker Property Management," she said, smiling at him. "We're just doing a quick walk-through of the house for the upcoming sale."

India groaned inwardly. She couldn't explain to Lucas about the sale of the house, without also revealing that she was the owner—at least not in front of Kim and Devin.

"Okay," she said brightly, grabbing her pocketbook from a nearby table. "We have to run, so I'll leave them in your capable hands, Mom."

"Have fun, darling," Joanna said.

Quickly, before Lucas could ask any questions, she caught his hand and pulled him out of the house.

"So, the owner is selling?" Lucas asked as they walked to his Jeep.

"Apparently," she agreed morosely. She disliked keeping the truth from Lucas, especially after everything they had shared, and considering how good he had been to her over the past several days. She waited until she was seated in the passenger's seat and they were driving down the mountain toward the lake before she drew in a deep breath and turned to him. "Listen, Lucas, there are some things you don't know about me, things I need to tell you."

His jaw worked, and India saw his hands tighten on the steering wheel. When he looked at her, his eyes were hidden behind his sunglasses, but she thought his smile seemed forced.

"We can talk over lunch," he said. "There are things I need to tell you, too."

His words, and the tone with which he said them, caused India's heart to clench in dread. Did he know her identity? Had he somehow spoken with the Howden family and figured it out? If so, he would despise her for not telling him the truth about herself right away. She was so absorbed in trying to figure out how she would explain to him, that she barely noticed the drive until they were pulling into the Snapdragon Inn parking lot. Lucas seemed preoccupied with his own thoughts, so if he noticed her silence, he made no comment.

"I told Mia we'd eat on the patio," Lucas said as he killed the engine. "We'll have a nice view of the lake."

He helped her climb out of the Jeep, and then she followed him up to the wide veranda and into the inn. India could smell something delicious cooking, and light, cheerful music filled the rooms, piped in through unseen speakers. She followed Lucas to the enormous dining room at the back of the inn, where floor to ceiling windows provided panoramic views of the mountains and lake. Beyond the windows, the large, circular stone terrace extended out over the lawn, and a dozen tables and umbrellas had been set up for guests.

"Oh, there you are!"

They turned to see Mia walk into the dining room from the kitchen, a welcoming smile on her face.

"Sit wherever you like, and I'll be right out," she said, indicating the patio.

They chose a small table nearest the lake, beneath a wide umbrella, and Mia came out and took their drink orders.

"I just made a beautiful blueberry lemonade," she said, smiling when India eagerly accepted. "And Lucas, I think I already know what you'll have. A beer, right?"

"You know me too well," Lucas said.

"Here's today's menu." Mia set a beautiful handwritten menu on the table between them. "Take your time."

India perused the abbreviated menu. "This all sounds so wonderful," she said. "I think I'll have the grilled lake trout and a salad." She glanced at Lucas. "What about you?"

"I'll have the same," he said, before he leaned back in his chair and laced his fingers across his flat stomach. "So, what is it you wanted to tell me?"

Disconcerted by his directness, India wasn't certain how to begin. If anything, he seemed more distant this morning than he had since she'd met him, and she felt suddenly hesitant.

"I wanted to talk to you about the other day, when we were together in your room." She couldn't read his expression, couldn't even tell if he was interested in what she had to say, or not. "Do you mind taking your sunglasses off? I can't talk to you like this."

"Just tell me, India." He suddenly sounded weary, but he pulled his glasses off and set them on the table. "Whatever it is."

His expression was shuttered, and India wondered if she only imagined his emotional withdrawal. He suddenly seemed like a stranger to her, as if they hadn't spent the previous afternoon making love in his room.

"Yesterday, when you wanted to know about the accident and the scars, I wasn't ready to talk about it," she said carefully. "But there are things you need to know, things I didn't tell you."

"I'm listening."

"I have no memory of the accident itself, or even of the weeks leading up to it," she said. She clutched her hands together on her lap. "I only know what the police and doctors have told me."

Lucas frowned. "You have no recollection of what happened?"

"None. The doctors said the memories might return, in time, but there's no guarantee."

"What about the driver of the car?"

"I already told you, he died at the scene."

"So you have no memory of where you were going, or why you were in the car with him to begin with?"

India shook her head. "No. I've gone through my calendar, but the only thing I had written down for that night was dinner with a girlfriend. She confirmed that we had dinner, and then we both caught a taxi home. At least she did. But that's not what I wanted to talk to you about. There's something else—"

He leaned forward. "Do you remember anything about the driver, or why you were together that night?"

"No." India's head began to throb, and she put her fingers to her temples and closed her eyes. This happened whenever she tried to force memories of that night. "I had dinner with a girlfriend on the night of the accident, but she said he wasn't there. I know his name, but I can't remember anything else about him. I don't even know how we knew each other!"

Reaching into his back pocket, Lucas withdrew his wallet. For a moment, India thought he was going to pay the bill and leave before they'd even eaten. Instead, he pulled out a folded piece of paper and began to smooth it out on the table between them.

"This is Martin Howden," he said, his voice low. "And that's you with him. You definitely knew each other, India. Do you remember how you met him, or why you were in the car with him?"

Taking the paper from him, India stared at it in growing confusion. Torn from *The New Yorker*, the glossy page had been folded so many times that the paper was in danger of disintegrating. But there was no mistaking the photo was of her and Martin Howden, walking beside each other. In the photograph, she wore the same dress she had worn the night of the accident.

She felt the blood drain from her face. "Where did you

get this?"

"Never mind that," Lucas said. "Are you certain you have no memories of Martin Howden?"

"I already told you!" she cried, shoving the page back toward him. "I didn't know him! I mean, it's true that at some point, I met up with Martin Howden and got into his car. But I have no idea why, or where we were going. That's the truth!"

From behind India, someone laughed, a harsh, brittle sound. "That's a load of royal B.S., darling, and you know it! Why don't you just admit that you were sleeping with Martin, and your little tryst that night turned tragic? At least for Martin, but not for you, it seems. Your life has turned out wonderful, hasn't it?"

India spun around in her chair even as Lucas shot to his feet, nearly knocking his chair over in the process. A woman stood several feet away, her chin high, dressed in a chic, white pantsuit. Her artfully dyed, blonde hair fell in expensive layers around her face, and her Hermès Birkin handbag alone was easily worth five figures. Now she pulled off her sunglasses, and pinioned India with a predatory look. As she walked closer, India could see she was older than she'd first realized, maybe in her mid-fifties. She looked familiar, but India couldn't place where she might have seen her before.

"Excuse me, do I know you?" she asked, standing up.

"India—" Lucas began, but the woman threw up a hand, forestalling whatever words he might have said.

"You don't know me, but I know you, sweetheart," the woman sneered, and stepped closer. "Martin Howden was my husband."

India's head began to spin, and she put a steadying hand on the back of her chair. Martin Howden's wife, Meredith! She had seen pictures of her before, but now her hairstyle looked different, and she'd lost weight.

"What are you doing here?" India asked, aware that her voice sounded faint.

She cast a helpless glance at Lucas, but he was staring at the other women with an intensity that bordered on dislike. India desperately wanted to go to him, assure him that the horrible things this woman said were absolutely untrue, that she would never have slept with Martin Howden. She felt sick to her stomach, nauseous with anxiety. This was not how she wanted Lucas to find out about the accident, or her involvement with the billionaire philanthropist. Now she turned back to Meredith Howden.

"How did you find me?"

The older woman gave her an unpleasant smile. "Why, hasn't Lucas told you? He's been tracking your movements since you left New York. His only purpose in coming to Glacier Creek was to uncover the truth about you and Martin—his father."

India gasped, and she whirled to face Lucas, waiting for him to deny it. He looked at Meredith and then her, and although India saw regret and anguish on his features, she also saw the truth.

"India," he said, and reached a hand toward her. "Maybe it started out like that, but it's not the way I feel now. Just please tell me you weren't in love with my stepfather—"

"You knew!" she breathed in horror, as the full implication of Meredith's words sank in. "All this time, you knew. You let me think you were interested in me, that you wanted a relationship with me, when all you really wanted was to find out if I'd been sleeping with Martin Howden?" She passed a hand over her eyes. "My God, I think I'm going to be sick."

Meredith walked up close to her, and for a brief instant, India thought the other woman intended to slap her. But she merely stared at her, sweeping her gaze over her as if she was some kind of interesting new insect.

"You look healthy. You still have your beauty and, presumably, your brains. So, what I really want to know is, what entitles you to a fifty-million-dollar settlement and the deed to the house here in Glacier Creek? A house that I now understand you intend to sell, although that doesn't surprise me." Her lip curled. "A mercenary creature like yourself can never have enough money, and you'll do whatever it takes to get more, isn't that right?"

"I don't have to listen to this," India said, and grabbed her pocketbook from where it hung on the back of her chair. "I'm sorry for your loss, but I'm leaving. If you have anything more to say to me, you can contact my lawyer."

"Do you deny you were sleeping with my husband?" Meredith demanded, but her voice broke on the last word.

India paused. Even in her own distress, she recognized the desperation in the other woman's voice. "I can't tell you anything about my relationship with your husband," she finally said. "I have no memory of it at all, except that I'm sure I did nothing to deserve your accusations. Now, if you'll excuse me—"

"That's right," Meredith said scornfully. "Run away. At least I arrived before you sank your hooks into my son!"

India practically ran across the patio to the stone steps that led to the grassy lawn, ignoring Lucas as he called her name. She didn't have a plan, only knew she needed to escape. Behind her, she heard Lucas talking in low, furious tones to his mother.

His mother!

God! She wanted to die of shame. She reached the grass and began walking swiftly across the property toward the road, not even glancing at Lucas's Jeep. She'd never accept a ride back to the house from him, not even if he begged.

"India, wait a minute, will you?" Lucas caught up with her and grabbed her wrist, which she tried unsuccessfully to snatch free.

"What?" she demanded, whirling to face him. "What is it you want from me, Lucas Talbot? If that's even your real name!"

"It is," he said. "Martin was my stepfather. I just wanted

to know more about you, India. I never intended to hurt you."

India looked at him in disbelief. "You wanted to know more about me? *Why?* Do you think I coerced your stepfather into sleeping with me, or somehow took advantage of him? Is that it? Do you think I manipulated that accident settlement, or had any say about how much money I received? Well, I didn't! I was in a coma, Lucas! *A coma!* For two months I lay in a hospital bed with a severe brain injury, while my mother didn't know if I would live or die! And when I finally did come out of the coma, it was another two months before I could leave the hospital! I did nothing wrong! I'm sorry about your stepfather, I really am. But I wasn't driving that night, and I'm not responsible for his death!"

"I know that," he said, his tone grim. "I don't know what to say except I'm sorry. I had no idea my mother was coming here. I was getting ready to tell you the truth about myself, and who I am, when she showed up."

India couldn't prevent a derisive snort. "Oh, really? Well, I was getting ready to tell you the truth about myself, too, but I've changed my mind. Now you'll never know."

Shaking his hand away, she turned and continued walking. Her chest and throat felt tight, and she knew tears weren't far behind.

"What truth, India?" Lucas asked. "What were you going to tell me?"

That I'm falling in love with you.

"That we have no future together, Lucas. We never did."

He stopped walking. She told herself she wouldn't look back at him, but she couldn't prevent glancing over her shoulder. His face looked anguished. She heard his hard exhalation of breath, and then he was beside her again.

"Let me drive you home," he said.

"Oh, you mean to *your* home? Your *family* home?" She gave a bitter laugh. "No wonder you knew all about the faulty circuit breaker, and I'm such an idiot I never put two and two together. I just believed everything you told me. God, I am so stupid!"

"I never lied to you."

India stopped then and turned to face him. He looked so handsome and so miserable, that for a moment she nearly flung herself against his chest. Instead, she crossed her arms around her middle.

"You lied by omission, Lucas."

"And what about you?" he asked. "You never told me you were the owner of the house. You deliberately let me think you were a friend of the Howden family."

"But you already knew the truth!" she said, laughing in disbelief. "You were the one deceiving me! I was just trying to keep a low profile. Do you know why I came to Glacier Creek in the first place? Because the paparazzi and the reporters wouldn't stop hounding me. I thought if I used an alias and came out here, maybe I could finally find some peace. But all I found was you—a liar and a master manipulator." She leaned forward. "Let me ask you, Lucas, did you mean to make me fall in love with you?"

His face cleared, and something like hope gleamed in his eyes. "You're in love with me?"

Too late, she realized what she'd said. "Of course not." She turned and began walking again. "Like I said, there was never any hope for us, you just didn't know that when you set out to spy on me."

To her astonishment, he caught her by the shoulders and dipped his head down to look into her eyes. "India, I am crazy about you. Nothing else matters. I don't care why you were in that car with my stepfather. I don't care about the money, or your reasons for selling the house. I love you!"

She stared at him in bemusement, even as her soft, stupid heart began to hammer hard against her ribs. But underlying the wonder of his admission, was the bitter reality of his betrayal. "How can you even talk about love, after what you did? You lied to me! You used a false pretext to get close to me in order to find out if I was *sleeping with your stepfather*! You used me in every way possible. How can I ever believe anything you say?"

"Because it's the truth," he insisted. Hectic color rode high on his cheekbones, and his eyes seemed impossibly green. "I know you can't remember what happened the night of the accident, but maybe it's better that way."

"Better for who? You?" She shrugged his hands away.

"It's too late. I don't want anything to do with you, Lucas Talbot."

Digging through her pocketbook, she pulled out her cell phone and punched in Katie's number.

"India, let's go somewhere and talk about this," Lucas persisted. "I know we can work this out."

"Absolutely not," she said, putting the mobile phone to her ear. "I never want to see you or talk to you again. Just think how relieved your mother will be."

"India—"

"We're done, Lucas. Good-bye." Turning, she walked away as tears welled in her eyes, and this time she didn't look back.

Chapter Fifteen

O NE WEEK HAD passed since his mother's unexpected
arrival at the Snapdragon Inn. A week of suffering and
self-recriminations for Lucas, who had done everything he
could think of to contact India. Her phone went directly to
voicemail, and no one answered the door at the mountain
house when he rang the bell. Both the house and the three-
car garage were empty. He knew, because he'd checked a half
dozen times. He had no idea where she was, or if she was
okay.

He couldn't stop thinking about her. Worrying about
her.

His mother had left on the next available flight to California, where she would spend the winter at her house in
Monterey. Lucas still couldn't believe how horribly wrong
that afternoon at the inn had gone. He'd had no idea his
mother intended to show up in Glacier Creek, or that she
would confront India in such an ugly way.

He blamed himself.

He hadn't been honest with either his mother or India.
He should have told his mother he wouldn't act as her spy,

especially after he'd met India and realized she wasn't the avaricious gold-digger his mother made her out to be. He should have told India who he was. Instead, he'd royally screwed up and alienated both women.

India was right; she had done nothing wrong. She'd been the victim in the accident, and he and his mother had only victimized her again. He'd driven his mother to the airport, and on the way he'd told her everything, leaving out only the parts where he'd slept with India. He'd told his mother he loved India, and that he intended to find her and make things right. Meredith's mouth had flattened in displeasure, but she hadn't argued with him.

Now he sat in a wooden Adirondack chair on the patio of the inn, and gloomily surveyed the lake and surrounding mountains. The trees had exploded with color, turning the hillsides into vibrant blankets of red, orange, and yellow. He thought India would have enjoyed the display.

"Well, I have to say you look pretty miserable."

Lucas glanced up to see Mia standing beside his chair. She had a glass of iced tea in each hand, and now she held one out to him. He accepted it gratefully.

"Thanks."

She sat down in the chair next to his and sipped her drink. "I couldn't help but overhear the conversation that day, when your mother arrived unannounced. I had no idea you were Martin Howden's stepson, or that India was the new owner of your family house."

"She is, yeah," he said. "But she deserves to have it. My family hasn't stayed in the house in over a decade. And if she wants to sell it, that's her prerogative."

"Hmm. I hear the house has been taken off the market," she said, her tone casual.

Lucas snapped his head up. "How did you hear that?"

Mia shrugged and gave him a secretive smile. "I have my sources. Actually, I ran into Kim Benatti, a local photographer. She's going to be covering a wedding we're hosting here in just a few weeks, and she happened to mention it in passing."

"Ah. Would that be Cole Tanner's wedding?"

"Yes. Do you know him?"

"Only slightly. But Lucas told me he was getting married here at the inn."

Mia smiled. "Yes. If anyone deserves a happy ending, it's Cole and Joy, and her sweet little girl, Piper." She considered Dylan for a moment. "You deserve that, too, whether you believe it or not."

After everything that had happened, Lucas doubted he deserved India, or a happy ending. But he was selfish enough to want it, and to try and have it.

"Did she say why the listing has been removed?"

"Something about the current owner wanting to convert it to a rehabilitation home for people recovering from traumatic head injuries." She smiled. "At least, that's what I think she said."

"If that's true, who would spearhead that kind of conversion?"

"Again, this is just hearsay, but Kim said India has been in talks with a team of doctors in New York City."

Was she in New York City?

"Are you sure?"

Mia shrugged. "I probably shouldn't be saying anything, but I saw her face that day when your mother showed up. If she's half as miserable as you are now, then you two need to get back together."

"If only that was possible."

Mia tipped her head. "Why isn't it?"

"Because I have no idea where she is."

"She's here in Glacier Creek," Mia said in surprise.

"What?"

Mia nodded, and her brow furrowed in concern. "I'm sorry, I thought you knew. Kim Benatti saw India's mother yesterday, in town."

He'd been to the house numerous times, only to find it empty. It was more than the fact nobody had answered the door; the timber-frame house had had a bleak, deserted feel to it. Nobody had been at home.

Lucas pushed his drink into Mia's hands.

"Thank you, Mia. I owe you!"

He pressed a swift kiss against her astonished face, and then he was sprinting to his Jeep. She was here. She hadn't left!

Now he thrust the Jeep into gear, churning gravel as he accelerated out of the parking lot and onto the lake road. His mind raced with everything he wanted to say to India. God, he'd been such an idiot. He only hoped he could convince her that they belonged together, and that none of the rest mattered. Even his mother would come around, eventually. She always did.

Ten minutes later, he pulled into the driveway of the timber-frame house and took the steps to the front door two at a time. Before he even had a chance to press the doorbell, the door opened. Katie stood there looking pale and tired, but her face brightened momentarily when she saw Lucas.

"I saw your Jeep pull up," she said, and stood back to let him in. "I know what happened and just for the record, I think what you did is absolute shit."

Lucas frowned. "I should have told her who I was right from the beginning. I'm sorry."

"If you had, I think she may have been freaked out at first, but she would have gotten over it. What you did, though—that was cruel."

"Can I see her? Will she see me?" He desperately needed to see her, to apologize again and then make it up to her however he could.

Katie's gaze shifted away from him. "She's not here. We moved into a hotel right after your—your argument. You're actually lucky to have caught me—I only came back here because I forgot something."

"Where are you staying?"

"I shouldn't tell you this, because she'll probably kill me, but India was hospitalized two days ago."

"*What?* What happened? Is she okay?" Images of India, sick or injured or worse, flashed through his mind.

"I'm heading over there now, so you can follow me if you want."

"Just tell me what happened, Katie."

When she looked at him, the utter bleakness of her expression caused Lucas's heart to stutter in fear. What could have happened to cause the look of desolation on Katie's face?

"Obviously, you know India was injured in the accident. But what you don't know—and what she was going to tell you that day at the inn—is that the car explosion left her with a tiny bit of shrapnel in her brain."

Lucas felt as if someone had kicked him hard in the gut. "So, what are you saying? Did they remove it?"

"No. She saw a bunch of different surgeons—all of them considered to be the best in their field—and all agreed it's inoperable. The fragment is too close to her brain stem and attempting to remove it could actually kill her."

Lucas stared at her, trying to comprehend her words. "What's her prognosis?"

Katie gave a helpless shrug, but Lucas didn't miss how her chin trembled. "That tiny bit of metal is like a ticking time bomb inside her head, and it could detonate anytime. If it shifts, she won't survive."

Lucas had lost buddies during his time in Afghanistan, Syria, and Yemen. He'd seen soldiers suffer horrific damage, including blast and fragment injuries, and he'd visited the widows and parents of those who had died. Each time, he'd been gutted by the loss, and it never got any easier. But hearing that India could die made his knees go rubbery, and his head feel light. He'd only just found her, and now he could lose her.

"Why is she in the hospital?" he managed to ask, and his voice sounded rough even to his own ears. "Is it the shrapnel?"

"She's had a migraine for almost a week, to the point where she can't eat or drink. Mom finally insisted on bringing her to the hospital. She's dehydrated, so they're treating her with fluids, but they also wanted to check the position of the shrapnel."

"I need to see her." He wasn't asking.

Katie looked at him for a moment, considering. "I don't want her upset."

"I don't want to upset her," Lucas assured her. "I want to tell her what a complete ass I've been, and to beg her forgiveness. Then I want her to understand just how much I love her."

After a moment, Katie nodded. "Okay. I'll meet you at the hospital."

Lucas followed the black Land Cruiser to the small hospital in Glacier Creek, his mind churning through the information that Katie had given him. India had suffered a severe head injury during the accident, and she still dealt with the effects daily. She'd tried to tell him that she couldn't recall anything about the accident or about Martin, before his mother had interrupted them and all but accused India of lying.

Lucas blew out a hard breath. He had so much to make up for. He only hoped it wasn't too late.

At the hospital, he followed Katie through the corridors until they arrived at India's room. The shades had been pulled and the lights were off, casting the small room in shadows. Joanna sat in a chair on the far side of the bed, scrolling through her smartphone. Now she looked up, and Lucas thought he saw both surprise and relief cross her face, before she quickly composed her features and stood up.

Lucas's gaze went to India. She looked wan and fragile. Her eyes were closed, her hands folded neatly over the blanket.

Joanna stopped by his side. "I'm glad you're here," she whispered. "She's been miserable since you argued." She glanced at India. "They gave her something for the pain, so she'll likely sleep for another hour or so."

"Do you mind if I wait with her?"

"Of course not. Katie and I will go get some lunch."

After they were gone, Lucas pulled the chair close to India's bed and studied her pale features. Even in the indistinct light, he could see the dark circles beneath her eyes, and noted the fine lines of pain on either side of her mouth.

Guilt tore at him.

This was his fault. If he'd only told her his true identity early on, he could have spared her his mother's ugly accusations. Maybe she wouldn't have wanted anything to do with him, but at least he wouldn't have caused her additional pain. Reaching out, he took her hand in his and curled his fingers around hers, as if he could infuse her with his own strength and good health. Her bones were slender and delicate, and he gently rubbed his thumb over her knuckles. Her breath hitched, and he looked up to see her eyes open. For a moment, her gaze was hazy and unfocused.

"Hey," he said softly.

She frowned and withdrew her hand from his. "What are you doing here? Where is my mother?"

"She and Katie went to get something to eat. How're you feeling?"

"Like a wrecking ball just crushed my skull. You shouldn't be here. I told you I don't want to see you."

Lucas winced. "I had to come. Why didn't you tell me about the shrapnel?"

She studied him for a moment, and then turned her face away. "I wanted to, but I didn't know how I could tell you about the accident without also telling you about Martin Howden. And how could I do that, when I don't remember anything about him?"

"You will remember," he assured her. "I believe your memory will return, and you'll realize you have nothing to hide. My stepfather was a generous man. He would want you to live your life to the fullest, India, in whatever way you can."

"So, you don't think we were sleeping together?"

Lucas heard the anxiety in her voice. "No, I don't." Even as he said the words, he realized it was the truth. He had allowed his mother's grief and anger to influence his own thoughts on what might have happened the night his stepfather had died. "Martin was never a philanderer. Maybe he and my mother weren't as close as she would have liked, but I believe he was faithful to her."

He didn't think his stepfather would have pursued India for a sexual relationship, and India didn't strike him as the kind of woman who either needed or wanted a sugar daddy. Eventually, they would learn why India had been in the car with Martin on that fateful night, but Lucas would stake his life on the fact that it wasn't for the reasons his mother believed.

"Your mother doesn't believe that."

"She's bitter and angry. For what it's worth, I'm sorry for the things she said to you. I had no idea she would be at the inn, and I'd give anything to take back what happened."

"I never wanted the money or the house," India said quietly. "That was all my lawyer's doing. I was a little horrified when I found out how much money I'd received, but my lawyer assured me the settlement had no monetary impact on Martin's family."

"And it didn't," Lucas assured her. "The mountain house was Martin's pride and joy. I loved the summers I spent here in Glacier Creek as a kid, but once I graduated college, I didn't return. I joined the military, and life got too busy. Martin's business ventures took up so much of his time that he didn't come back, either. My mother always preferred the Hamptons or Monterey to Montana, so I know she never missed the house. It's been sitting mostly empty for the past ten years."

"I'm not keeping it," she said quietly.

"Yes, I heard," Lucas said. Reaching out, he captured her hand again, and this time she didn't resist. "I think turning the house into a rehab center for people with traumatic head injuries is a great idea."

"You do?"

Lucas nodded. "I have buddies who still struggle with PTSD, and I've seen my share of blast injuries. What better place to heal than here, in Glacier Greek?"

India smiled wanly. "That's what I thought, too. And I wouldn't want them to pay anything to come here. All costs would be covered."

"I have plenty of resources, and Martin had a charitable organization for just this kind of venture. I know he would approve of using the house for this purpose. You should apply for funding to bring in the best doctors and staff."

"Lucas," she said, her tone wry. "I have fifty million dollars, remember?"

"You need to keep that money," he said.

"Somehow, I don't think I'm going to need it."

Her words caused alarm bells to jangle in his head. "What are you talking about? I know about the shrapnel in your head, India. We'll find a doctor who can safely remove it."

India shook her head. "No, it's not possible. I've already consulted with some of the best neurosurgeons in the country. The shrapnel is inoperable."

Lucas looked at her with tender exasperation. "Is that why you told me we never had a chance? Because you think you're going to die?"

The expression on India's face twisted his heart. "I don't hold out much hope for a long and happy life, Lucas."

Lucas smiled then. Reaching out, he stroked the back of his fingers gently along her jaw. "But you didn't count on me, India. Maybe you haven't realized, but I'm a pretty stubborn guy. I love you, and I won't settle for anything but a long and happy life, together."

India's eyes filled with tears, but she gave him a wobbly smile. "I may have lied when I told you I never wanted to see you again."

"I know," he said, and kissed her.

Chapter Sixteen

LUCAS SAT IN the small waiting room inside a renowned New York City hospital, his head in his hands. India's mother and sister sat in the chairs next to him, and on the other side of the room, Jamie and Dylan stood in quiet conversation with Rachel and Hayden.

"How long has it been?" Joanna asked, breaking into his thoughts.

Lucas heard the fear in her voice, and he understood. He'd been a mass of nervous energy since India had gone into surgery. Now he glanced at his watch.

"It's been six hours."

"The surgeons said the operation should take no more than four hours," Katie said, her eyes clouded with concern. "What if something went wrong?"

"They would have come out to tell us," Lucas said, and hoped he was right. "We knew the surgery would take time. She has a great team of surgeons in that room with her, and I have to believe she'll be okay."

Anything less would be unacceptable.

Unthinkable.

"I don't know how to thank you for doing this for us," Joanna said.

Lucas nodded. He hadn't done it for Joanna or for Katie. He'd done it for himself and India, to give them the best chance of a future together.

After he'd learned about the shrapnel in India's brain, he'd contacted his stepfather's charitable organization. Martin Howden had been an intelligent, inquisitive, and generous man who had donated vast amounts of money to various cutting-edge technologies. His connections in the medical field spanned the globe. Drawing on the respect Martin had commanded during his life, Lucas had organized a virtual meeting that included thirty of the most esteemed neurosurgeons in the world. They had reviewed India's medical records, had consulted amongst themselves, and then three of them had come forward to say they believed India's shrapnel could be removed.

India had been unwilling to even consider undergoing surgery, until the three surgeons had flown to Glacier Creek to perform a physical examination. Together with Lucas and her mother and sister, they had finally convinced her to undergo the lifesaving operation. She had flown by private jet to New York, where she had undergone three days of tests, before the surgery had finally been scheduled.

"I'll check with the desk to see if they've had any updates," Katie offered, pushing to her feet. "I don't know how much longer I can sit here, doing nothing. I have to know."

Lucas understood. He felt like he was slowly going crazy, and he had to force himself not to let his imagination run riot. He couldn't even consider the possibility that India wouldn't survive the surgery.

She had to.

"Here comes Dr. Gratz!" Katie shot to her feet, swiping her hands nervously on the seat of her pants. Joanna put her arm around her daughter's shoulders as they watched the neurosurgeon approach.

Lucas stood up. He tried to read the surgeon's expression as he walked toward them, but his face was inscrutable.

"How is she?" Katie asked, as soon as the doctor entered the waiting area.

"I'm happy to report she came through the surgery with flying colors."

Joanna stifled a sob and turned to hug Katie. "Thank God!"

A wave of relief washed over Lucas, so powerful that for a moment he thought he might need to sit down again. But a part of him recognized the doctor didn't smile or offer any other words of assurance.

"Is she out of the woods?" Lucas asked.

"The next twenty-four hours are critical," Dr. Gratz said. "Once she's conscious, we'll perform an evaluation to ensure she didn't suffer any neurological damage. But the shrapnel is out, she's breathing on her own, and we're confident there's no damage to her brain stem. Provided there's no excessive brain swelling or infection, I expect her to make a full recovery."

"Thank you," Joanna said, and impulsively hugged the doctor. "She's strong. I know she'll be okay."

"Can we see her?" Katie asked.

"She's heavily sedated, so she won't know you're there," the doctor warned. "But yes, you can see her."

Lucas deliberately hung back, allowing Joanna and Katie to follow the doctor to India's room. He desperately wanted to see her, to assure himself that she was alive, but he understood that he had no rights where she was concerned. He wasn't family.

Nearly thirty minutes passed before they returned. Lucas thought both women looked weary, but hopeful.

"I'm going to bring Mom back to the hotel, and we're both going to get some sleep," Katie said, smiling. "India looks remarkably good."

"I'll go in and sit with her," Lucas said. "If she wakes up, she won't be alone."

She wouldn't be alone ever again, if he could help it. She had been moved from recovery to a private room, and although she was still hooked to several monitors, Lucas was relieved to see how good she looked, considering she had just come through major surgery. Her head was swathed in white bandages, with a compression netting over it to hold it in place. Pulling a chair close to her bedside, he made himself comfortable, and settled in to wait.

A LIGHT TOUCH on his arm brought him out of an unsettled sleep, and Lucas came awake with a start, momentarily disoriented. He was still sitting by India's bedside, and her eyes were open as she watched him. He hadn't meant to fall asleep, and now he glanced at his watch, dismayed to see it was nearly six o'clock in the morning. He'd managed to stay awake until midnight, when weariness had finally done him in.

"Hey," he said gently, leaning forward with a smile. "How're you feeling?"

"Parched," she managed to croak. "My throat is sore."

"Here, think you can swallow some water?" He was so relieved that she was awake and coherent, that his hand trembled as he poured a glass of water for her, slipped a straw in, and then held it to her lips. She took several small sips and nodded.

"Thanks," she managed. "How did the surgery go?"

"Like clockwork." He lifted her hand and pressed a kiss against her palm. "They removed the shrapnel, and said you'll make a full recovery."

"Are you sure? You're telling the truth?"

"I'll never lie to you again, baby."

"Oh, Lucas…"

"Hey," he said gently, and used his thumb to sweep away a tear as it rolled down her cheek. "Why are you crying?"

She smiled, and then laughed through her tears. "Because I'm happy. Because I never would have had the surgery if it wasn't for you. Because for the first time since the accident, I feel as if I have a chance at a future."

"Ah, sweetheart, you definitely have a future. I only hope there's a place in that future for me?"

"You have to ask?"

Although India had forgiven him for his deception, that had been before the surgery when she still believed she might die young. But now that her future looked bright, she could have any guy she wanted.

"Maybe you shouldn't talk right now," he said. "Get some sleep."

"No, I have to say this. When I learned why you had come to Glacier Creek, and why you were so interested in getting to know me, I was devastated, because I had already fallen in love with you."

"Ah, babe, I was a goner the first time I saw you in that shop." Lucas swallowed hard. "Maybe my original intentions weren't admirable, but it didn't take me long to realize I was falling in love with you. I wanted to tell you the truth so many times, but I was afraid of losing you."

"Oh, Lucas," she said softly.

"I believe there's a reason we both ended up in Glacier Creek," he continued. "Hell, I think there's a reason why you were in that car with Martin on the night of the accident. We were meant to be together, India."

"I wanted to tell you about Martin," she said. "But at that point, I had no memories of him, or why we were in the car that night."

Lucas sharpened his gaze on her. "What do you mean, at that point? Are you saying you remember?"

"I've begun to remember some things," she confirmed. "It's all still hazy, but I recall being in the car. It was raining that night. I had just had dinner with a friend in Manhattan, and I was standing outside the restaurant trying to get a taxi."

"You remember that?"

"Yes, and I remember Martin. He'd had dinner with several clients at the same restaurant and was waiting for the valet service to bring his car around for him."

"He had a personal driver, but he loved driving that sports car," Lucas confirmed.

"Yes, we got chatting while we were both waiting. I introduced myself, and he said he knew who I was, which surprised me."

The news didn't surprise Lucas. His stepfather had made it a point to know everyone who was anyone in New York City. As a media mogul, he would have watched India's meteoric rise in the magazine industry with interest.

"Did he offer to drive you home?"

"He did. I refused, of course, but he said he wanted to talk about my career. He invited me for a cup of coffee in Midtown. It was still early, and I knew who he was, so I accepted." She looked at Lucas and he saw the concern in her eyes. "He wasn't remotely interested in me in that way."

"I believe you. What else do you remember?"

"That's all," she admitted, looking sad. "I remember getting into the car, but nothing else."

"Well, that's something," he said, and gave her an encouraging smile. "It proves you didn't know him before that night, and that you weren't romantically involved with him."

"I never believed I was, but since I couldn't remember anything, I could never be sure."

"I don't want you to worry about anything," Lucas said. "You need to get some rest now. If the doctor realizes how much talking you've done, he won't let me visit again."

"You asked me once if I trust you, and I want you to know that I do. If I remember anything else, I'll tell you, no matter what it is."

Reaching out, Lucas curled his fingers around hers. "Sweetheart," he said, "I just want you to get better. I know we've moved very fast, and I'm more than willing to slow things down, if that's what it takes to make you feel comfortable. We have time to do this right."

India smiled, and it transformed her face. "Yes. Finally, we have time."

Chapter Seventeen

One Year Later

"ARE YOU READY?" Lucas asked.

He and India stood in the entry of the timber-frame house in Glacier Creek. Outside, a dozen or more reporters stood waiting, their cameras and microphones ready. More than three hundred people from the town had assembled in the newly constructed parking lot while local food vendors provided free food and drinks, and a small band performed on the lawn.

"I can't believe we did it," India said, and drew in a deep breath.

"You did it, babe, not me," Lucas corrected her. "You had the vision to turn this house into something special, and you did."

"I couldn't have done this without you," she said. "You were the one who contacted Martin's associates and got the financial backing to make it happen."

Once India had shared her dream with Lucas, he had made it his mission to solicit donations from his stepfather's charitable organization, as well as Martin's wealthiest associates. After the necessary modifications had been made to the house, they had raised enough money to ensure the new rehabilitation center could remain operational for the next twenty years, at least.

Lucas gave her a tender look. "You donated almost fifty million dollars, India."

India had used the money from her accident settlement to underwrite the construction of a new wing at the small, Glacier Creek hospital, and also build a small condominium complex near the outskirts of town, so that families could stay near their loved ones while they recuperated. Built on the side of a mountain, each unit had three bedrooms and a view of the lake, and a shuttle provided daily transportation between the apartments and the Martin Howden House. Now she took Lucas's hand and smiled at him, letting the love she felt for him show in her eyes.

"I never wanted the money," she said. "I have everything I've ever wanted, right here with you."

Lucas lifted her hand and pressed a kiss against her palm. Sunlight caught the facets on the solitaire diamond ring she wore and cast glittering pinpoints of light across her blouse.

"You are so beautiful," he said. "Inside and out, and I'm the luckiest son of a bitch on the planet to have found you."

"Are you certain you want me to talk about your stepfather? To share what I remember about him?"

"I think we owe him that," Lucas said. "Your memories have returned, and now we know why you were in the car with him, and what happened that night."

India drew in a deep breath and let it out slowly. "Okay. I can do that. Has your mother arrived yet?"

"I haven't seen her, but she'll be here."

His twin sisters had arrived more than a week ago and, along with Katie, had thrown themselves into the preparations for the grand opening. The three girls had become good friends over the past year, and India enjoyed seeing them laughing together. Both Lily and Natalie had transferred to a new college together, and seemed to be adjusting well. She knew Lucas was relieved to see them doing so much better than they had been a year ago.

"I'm just glad your mother no longer hates me," India said, grimacing.

"I think she feels the same way," Lucas said. "She wanted to pay for the entire wedding, she felt so miserable about what she did."

"I'm glad we're having a simple ceremony," India said with feeling. "And I can't imagine a better place to start our lives together, than right here in Glacier Creek."

Reaching out, Lucas tucked a stray tendril of hair behind her ear. "I agree."

Her hair had grown in the past year, and her corkscrew curls hung nearly to her shoulders. Knowing how much Lucas loved them, she had opted to grow her hair long again, the way it had been before her accident. Lucas had proposed six months ago, and the wedding would take place on

Christmas Eve, at the Snapdragon Inn.

She and Lucas had attended the wedding of Cole Tanner and Joy Holliday a year earlier, at the inn. The ceremony had been simple and beautiful, and Mia Davies had transformed the inn and the surrounding grounds into something truly magical. India couldn't think of a more perfect spot for her and Lucas to exchange vows. After the ceremony, they would move into their new home, which was still under construction just up the road from the Martin Howden House.

Now India looked out over the people assembled in front of the house. They had come to celebrate the opening of the Martin Howden House, a residential treatment center for traumatic brain injury. She and Lucas had worked tirelessly during the past year to make her dream a reality. The house had eight beds, and a fully equipped physical therapy room in the lower level. A staff of specialists stood ready to provide a full range of services around the clock. The first patients would arrive before the end of the week, including a former soldier from Lucas's unit in Yemen.

Dr. Gratz, the surgeon who had performed her surgery, came to stand beside them. He'd been instrumental in putting India in touch with people in the medical field who had helped make her dream a reality, and she had insisted he come to Glacier Creek for the grand opening of the center.

"Are you ready to cut the ribbon?" he asked.

India drew in a deep breath, trying to quell her sudden nerves. "We are."

"You're saving a lot of lives," he said quietly.

India gave him a fond look. "You're the one who saves lives," she said.

"This place will provide patients with the coping mechanisms they need to live a full and productive life."

As they stepped closer to the ribbon that stretched across the entrance of the house, the band began to play and the throngs of people drew closer. Dr. Gratz held up his hands, smiling and expressing his thanks, until the music finally stopped.

"Thank you, everyone, for coming out on this beautiful day to celebrate the opening of the Martin Howden House, a place of refuge and renewal," he said. "I'm thrilled to have been a part of this venture, and I'm excited about the difference this center is going to make for so many people. Now I'd like to introduce Ms. India Gale, the beauty and the brains behind this amazing operation."

India felt herself flush with pleasure as she stepped forward, pulling Lucas with her. "Thank you, Dr. Gratz. I'm very moved to be here today, to see how joyously my vision of caring has been realized. Some of you know that two years ago I was involved in a serious car accident—the same accident that took Martin Howden's life. Although I didn't know Martin very well, what I've learned about him over the past year has confirmed my belief that he was a man of great compassion and great vision. He loved this house, and he loved Glacier Creek. I think he would approve of what we've done here today."

She waited as the crowd applauded.

"For more than a year, I had no memories of the accident, or of Martin Howden. Martin was kind enough to offer me a ride home that night, but he suffered a medical emergency while we were driving."

India paused, feeling her throat tighten as she recalled the events of that night. Lucas put his arm around her shoulders and gave her an encouraging hug.

"Before the accident, we talked briefly about his generosity in supporting various charities, and I believe supporting those causes gave him great pleasure. Today's ribbon-cutting ceremony is dedicated to Martin Howden and to his amazing legacy. If you believe with all your heart, and work with all your might, dreams do come true. I'm so happy that we're going to make dreams come true for so many deserving people."

The crowd clapped as Dr. Gratz handed India an oversized pair of scissors. Together, she and Dr. Gratz and Lucas placed their hands on the handles, and together they cut the wide ribbon that stretched across the porch. As the ends fluttered away, a cheer went up from the crowd and the band began to play once more.

"Welcome to the Martin Howden House!" India declared.

Beaming with pleasure, she turned to Lucas and kissed him as the music swelled around them. Life was sweeter than she had ever believed possible. As they broke apart and turned toward the crowd, she saw her mother and sister standing near the steps, smiling broadly. Beside them stood Meredith Howden, wearing a long, cable-knit sweater in a gorgeous shade of blue and a pair of wide-legged pants and boots. She climbed the steps to where India and Lucas stood, and gave them each a quick kiss.

"Congratulations," she said. "Martin would be so proud."

"I'm glad you could make it, Mom," Lucas said, keeping his arm around India.

"I suppose I'll learn to like Montana," she teased, her voice overly dramatic. "Especially if my future grandchildren are going to be raised here!"

"We're having a beautiful in-law suite built into the new house," India said. "I think you'll like it."

"Darling," Meredith replied, "I'm going to love it. Thank you so much for including me in your life. It's more than I deserve."

Astonished, India saw a sheen of tears in the older woman's eyes, and an unexpected surge of sympathy washed over her.

"Don't mind me," Meredith said, laughing and flapping a hand. "I'm feeling unaccountably emotional today, but I have some fabulous news for you, India."

India's mother, Joanna, joined them on the porch, and now she gave India a secretive smile. "You're going to love this."

"I am?" India asked in surprise. She couldn't imagine what news Meredith might have.

"I've been working on my own charitable project for the past year or so," she said. "My husband was a great patron of the arts, and he loved nothing better than to help a young artist launch his or her career. He saw something in you, India, a talent that he wanted to promote."

"Martin actually talked about India?" Lucas said, frowning. "What did he say, and why didn't you mention this before?"

"Because I'm a foolish woman," she said, her voice rich with self-loathing. "He spoke of India several times before his death, but only in a professional manner. I see that now, but I was so distressed over his passing that I was willing to believe the worst of him. And of you."

"I was so surprised when he told me he knew who I was," India murmured. "We spent such a short amount of time together, and we mostly talked about his charities. But just before the accident—he said he wanted me to come work for him, to be part of his media group."

"He was so impressed with the work you did as the creative director for *Brazen Magazine*. Your meeting each other that night must have felt very serendipitous to him. He did want you to come work for him."

India felt her throat tighten with emotion. So much misunderstanding and misdirected anger as a result of her memory loss. Would she have accepted the job? And if she had, would she have eventually met Lucas?

"You see?" he murmured in her ear, reading the direction of her thoughts. "It was all meant to happen."

"I wanted to do something meaningful," Meredith continued. "Therefore, in his memory and to support his love of the arts, a community arts center will open next year in downtown Glacier Creek." She paused. "I'm hopeful that you'll agree to be the new director."

India stared at the other woman in astonishment. "You did that?"

Meredith looked only slightly smug. "I did. Well, with a little help from Lucas."

Lucas looked both embarrassed and pleased. "We purchased some empty space in the mercantile building, so the arts center will actually be right next door to *Adrenaline Adventures.*"

"The interior is stunning," Meredith gushed, "with plenty of light, high ceilings, and all the necessary facilities. You could run art classes, pottery classes, or even open a gallery. Whatever you think best."

India was speechless. "I'm overwhelmed," she finally managed to say. "And yes, I would love to run the arts center! Doing something like that has been a dream of mine for a long time. I loved working for the magazine, but I always wanted to work in a small town, with other people who loved art as much as I do. I could ask Hayden to come work there with me!"

"Then consider this my wedding gift to you," Meredith said, in satisfaction.

On impulse, India hugged the other woman. "Thank you so much."

"Oh, darling, do be careful! You'll smudge my makeup!" But she smiled as she pulled away. "I'm sure you both have tons of people to mingle with, so I think I'll go inside and make myself a martini. I seem to recall there's a lovely view from the back deck."

"I think I'll join you," said Joanna. She linked her arm with Meredith's and accompanied her into the house.

India turned to Lucas, and they both burst out laughing. "This day just keeps getting better," she said, when she could speak.

"Are you happy about the arts center?" Lucas asked. "She really wanted to do something special for you, to make up for what she did—what we both did—last year. She never told me that Martin knew who you were, or that he expressed an interest in your career, but it doesn't surprise me. I would have told you if I'd known."

"Lucas, we never have to talk about that again," India assured him. "I think you're right; we were meant to be together."

Lucas pulled her into his arms. "I'm glad you were with him at the end," he said. "I think he'd be happy to see us together."

"Martin Howden saved my life," India said.

Lucas frowned. "How do you mean?"

India dragged in a shaky breath. "I had another memory come back, recently. I wasn't going to tell you because I don't want to upset you, but I remember everything that happened that night."

"Martin had a diabetes attack," Lucas said gently. "None of what happened was your fault. What do you mean, he saved your life?"

"While we were talking, he started getting confused. He wasn't making any sense and his speech began to slur. I remember wondering if he'd had too much to drink and I just hadn't noticed. I didn't realize he was suffering a sugar low. Then he collapsed against the wheel with his foot on the gas pedal. I tried to grab the wheel, but I couldn't move him."

"Shh," Lucas murmured against her hair. "You don't need to do this."

"No," she persisted. "I do. You see, after we crashed into the pole and the car caught fire, he came around."

Lucas pulled back enough to search her eyes. "The autopsy report said he likely never regained consciousness."

India shook her head. "No, that's not true. The car was filling with smoke, and I couldn't breathe. I undid my seat belt and tried to open my door, but it was jammed. I was trapped. That's when Martin grabbed me, and pointed to his window, which was rolled down. Lucas, he all but dragged me over the center console. I had to crawl across him to get out the window, and he helped me. He pushed me free of the car!"

"Then why didn't he free himself?"

India shook her head. "I don't think he could get out. The sports car was so small and the driver's seat was so tight, and the steering wheel was in his way. I couldn't open his door. I reached through the window and tried to pull him out, but it was no use. I ran toward the street to wave someone down, and that's when the car exploded. I'm so sorry."

"Oh, India," Lucas murmured, and tightened his arms around her. "I'm so sorry."

"He saved my life," she said, her voice muffled against his chest. "If it wasn't for him, I would have died in that car. His first thought was to save me, not himself." Lifting her head, she searched his eyes. "Was I right to tell you? Would you rather not have known?"

"No," Lucas assured her. "I'm glad you told me. That sounds exactly like something Martin would do. He wanted you to survive, to live your life."

India nodded. Her throat was tight with suppressed emotion. She owed Martin Howden so much more than just the second chance he had given her. She owed him her happiness.

She owed him everything.

"He saved me a second time when you came into my

life," she continued softly. "Following the accident, I met with a dozen different doctors who said the shrapnel was inoperable. But your stepfather had so many colleagues and friends in the medical industry that I feel as if he guided Dr. Gratz to you. If it wasn't for your persistence, Dr. Gratz never would have agreed to even look at my case."

He dragged in a deep breath, and India could see how much her words affected him. "I think Martin is watching over us," he finally said. "And wherever he is, I think he's smiling."

"I love you, Lucas Talbot," she said, and she kissed him with all the love she felt.

"I'm going to spend the rest of my life showing you how much I love you," Lucas said.

Putting an arm around her shoulders, he hugged her tight against his side, as they turned and entered the Martin Howden House to start their lives together.

The End

The Glacier Creek Series

Book 1: *A Hot Montana Summer*

Book 2: *The Firefighter's Slow Burn*

Book 3: *A Soldier's Homecoming*

Available now at your favorite online retailer!

About the Author

Karen Foley admits to being an incurable romantic. When she's not working for the Department of Defense, she loves writing sexy stories about alpha heroes and strong heroines. Karen lives in New England with her husband, two daughters, and a houseful of pets.

Thank you for reading

A Soldier's Homecoming

If you enjoyed this book, you can find more from all our great authors at TulePublishing.com, or from your favorite online retailer.

TULE
PUBLISHING

Made in the USA
Columbia, SC
09 July 2018